BARBRO KARLÉN was bc
book *Man on Earth*, publi
the best-selling poetry book of all time in C
the next 5 years, 9 further volumes of her prose and
poetry were published. She worked as a mounted
policewoman for 18 years, and has trained and com-
peted in equestrian dressage for over 30 years. Her
autobiography *And the Wolves Howled* has recently been
published.

WHEN THE STORM COMES

A MOMENT IN THE BLOSSOM KINGDOM

'When the Storm Comes'. From the cover of the original Swedish edition, 1972.

WHEN THE STORM COMES

A MOMENT IN THE BLOSSOM KINGDOM

BARBRO KARLÉN

CLAIRVIEW

Clairview Books
An imprint of Temple Lodge Publishing
Hillside House, The Square
Forest Row, East Sussex
RH18 5ES

www.clairviewbooks.com

First published by Clairview 2001

Translated from Swedish by Jane Luxford

Originally published in Swedish as two separate books:
En stund i Blomrike by Wezäta Förlag, Göteborg 1969
and *När stormen kom* by Zindermans, Göteborg 1972

A catalogue record for this book is available from the
British Library

ISBN 1 902636 23 6

Cover by Andrew Morgan Design
Typeset by DP Photosetting, Aylesbury, Bucks.
Printed and bound by Cromwell Press Limited,
Trowbridge, Wilts.

CONTENTS

PUBLISHER'S FOREWORD

Barbro Karlén has recently been introduced to the English-speaking world through her autobiography, *And the Wolves Howled, Fragments of Two Lifetimes.* The two books published within this volume, however, were written many years ago—the first when Barbro was aged 10, and the second when she was 12. At that time, in the late 1960s, she had become known in her native Sweden as something of a literary sensation—a bestselling child author who had the ability to write beautiful and inspired prose and poetry. Although in more recent times there has been some controversy surrounding Barbro Karlén over her published memories of a previous life as a well-known figure connected with the Second World War, it is important to note that at the time these books were first made available her memories were quite private, and her work was published and sold purely on its literary merit.

The publication of these works in the English language—some 30 or more years after the original editions in Swedish–is long overdue. They are testimony to the truly remarkable abilities of an inwardly lonely but extraordinarily gifted child. But they are not noteworthy simply because a young child wrote them; they hold their own beside any 'adult' writing. The author of the original foreword to 'A Moment in the Blossom Kingdom' wrote: '…ultimately Francis of Assisi could have written this psalm of the immortality of the soul. Paul's letter to the Corinthians also springs to mind … [Barbro] has given us star dust.'

These two books constitute a warning from the world of the 'child' to the world of the 'adult'. The message is loud and clear: it is time to change before catastrophe strikes. The increasing number of natural disasters around the world, the adverse signs of global warming and the changes in weather patterns all suggest not only that her prophetic warnings were accurate, but also that unfortunately they have not been acted upon.

In 'A Moment in the Blossom Kingdom' young Barbro invites the reader to a fairy tale kingdom, where the prerequisite for entering is to be 'childlike'; but this is not tweeness or sticky-sweet sentimentality. Rather, we are asked to find a pure and untainted higher quality in ourselves. One is reminded of Christ's words in the Gospel: 'I tell you the truth, unless you change and become like little children, you will never enter the kingdom of heaven.' (Matthew 18:3)

With regard to the language, it should be noted that the punctuation in this volume follows that of the original; for example the author rarely used quotation marks, prefacing most reported speech only with a dash. Also, in many instances her phrases are unusual but characteristic, and so have been retained. Although the verses in the original were all in rhyme, it has not always been possible to reproduce the same effect in English.

We are grateful to Jane Luxford for the gift of her translation. Barbro Karlén, who is fluent in English, has personally checked and revised the English text.

SG, May 2001

WHEN THE STORM COMES

Over the crowns of the green trees
a mighty space is seen
Time's narrow path disappears
Eternity is not hidden
Immeasurable love
streams to a reawakened forest
Nature's own voice speaks
Little Earth hear my word

Hear how in peace I call you
forest and fields, town and land
I, Nature, only give freedom
far away from force and restraint
take from the Earth all which nourishes
and which I, Nature, have humbly given
look at the trees and flowers
how they smile at each other

They share the little green hill
They share a little plot
Look at the little blue violet
How she curtsys before the dandelion
See how the large proud fir
shields the little lonely linden tree
See how playful the little wind of spring
dried the tears on the cheek of the blossom

Listen, now hear the twittering birds
Nature's child has just awoken
Calls her mate and soon gets a reply
In great love they build their nest
Soon the little ones will be there
They will teach the Earth inhabitants
how to live their lives

They will teach us that freedom
is not something that one takes
Freedom is in the secret of eternity
Freedom is the reply from Nature
But we must be able to love
every straw and blade of grass
Listen now little human being
to the prayer that Nature prayed

Human, human being, feel your responsibility
Don't rush forward like a wild animal
Do you know why animals became wild?
Human beings captured them in cages
It went against the laws of Nature
when they devastated land and forest
Hear how wise Nature now whispers
poor Earth you have suffered enough

All seas will soon be poisoned
by all the waste from human hands
Poison spreads with the wind
all over the devastated land
The air continually polluted
Oxygen is lessened day by day
when human beings don't understand
that they attacked the law of Nature

Then Nature turns in force
Takes all its wisdom with it
and puts everything in its right place
Straightens everything that has gone askew
Humans terrifyingly will see
how Nature revolts
It will show the people of the Earth
the danger when you disturb Nature

But, little children
Nature says, the judgement
will not come yet
There is time for you to rethink
Do not poison the senses of Nature
Live in complete love with me
then I shall not fight back cruelly
and let loose all my forces

So in the still night spoke
wise Nature to the child of the Earth
Little child who listened in stillness
remember these words of wisdom
The child stretched forth her hands
and embraced the soul of Nature
Nature and child enfolding one another
whispered—all shall be well!

The crown of the tree rustled. The birds were cowering in the thick branches, perceiving imminent danger. The people on the Earth were hurrying, everyone in their own direction. Bad weather was on its way. Large dark masses of clouds chased each other across the sky. The storm, hard and ruthless, swept forward. Not like an ordinary storm. It was Nature who had declared war on the inhabitants of the Earth. Nature had put up with all the unfairness that people had enacted towards it. Nature had felt it would soon lose the struggle and become extinct itself if it did not show human beings their weakened position in the universe.

Long enough had patient Nature seen how human beings became worse and worse. But now this patience had come to an end. Nature thought, I will start by sending storms across the evil Earth. I want to see if human beings will perhaps understand that I am the strongest. Maybe it's enough just to reshuffle things a bit between forest, valleys, streets, fields and human dwellings. But I have to take care over how I do this, thought the highly strained Nature, so that I don't damage the animals and plants too much. But they have promised to sacrifice part of themselves to help me show human beings their place on the Earth. For human beings have poisoned most of the Earth, and even themselves. They have poisoned the air, a large part of the land and the sea. Therefore, Nature has prepared for this war for a long time; the war the people of the Earth have asked for. With great sorrow in its soul, Nature sees how scared the little birds are, how they have hidden themselves in the deepest forests. Some forest I will save for you, little children of the heights, who have never done any harm.

The storm grew worse and worse. People ran like frightened mice and hid from falling trees, roofs and loose planks, which were ripped off from everywhere. Human beings were frightened and began to feel their own littleness. Nature was glad. 'Maybe I don't have to use any more violence. Maybe the small people will understand how dangerous it is to go against my laws.'

The storm abated and both animals and humans came out of their hiding places. Yes, everyone was glad that the storm was finished. But had the human beings learnt anything? No, nothing at all! They continued to make war and destroy each other and continued to spread poison over the world.

With sorrow in its heart, Nature had to use stronger power to show human beings who holds sway over the universe.

Nature was the highest ruler of the whole universe. It obeyed directly the greatest of the worlds.

But how should one go about straightening up all these calamities that were getting worse and worse? The trees which were blown down were used for many different purposes. It wasn't wrong precisely, but it wasn't what was meant.

The houses, which had been razed by the hard storms, were built up again. Some people hit by the falling trees and other things flying around had been so badly hurt that they left the Earth. But not even that seemed to make a difference. It didn't have significance. It was acceptable to replace those who had fallen away. Often those who came were worse than those who had gone.

But how shall Nature act to reach right into the innermost kernel of the Earth beings? Nature, which only meant well towards everything, wanted to tell the thoughtless humans how they could be the best of friends, both with each other and all the forces around them.

Nature is neither he, she, nor it. That's why it's so difficult to give a name to Nature. If I should translate what Nature really is I could only say, 'It's like the feeling of mighty powers.' Just like human's, animal's and plant's feelings cannot be described as male or female.

Now, thought Nature: I will ask the Earth for help. Maybe she can help to bring order to the awkward Earth dwellers. Surely it was both terrible and sad to be forced to use all kinds of ways to get order.

At first the Earth was a little doubtful, but agreed when Nature said that the Earth could get rid of many, or maybe all, of its prisons and other terrible things.

But how shall we do it, the Earth wondered.

And then Nature began to explain.

Earth, said Nature, you know how much blood has flowed into you, both from humans and animals. You also know that human beings have you as a home but they argue and fight with each other. Hardly anyone shares with each other. Everyone fights for power. People have difficulty keeping the peace. Nearly everyone has forgotten the meaning of life on Earth. They have had a long time in which to find order in their thoughts; they have been given sense and free will, but how have they used them?

Yes, mostly to hoard the best for themselves. They have put up all kinds of laws and rules which are completely foreign to me. Now, for their own good, they must see their own lack of knowledge, in face of the highest eternal universe. We must show them how the laws of Nature really work. It is entirely wrong that there are lords and slaves on the Earth. No one is greater than the other.

Everyone is created by the same high power. Everyone has a right to a part of the riches of the Earth, yet human beings have divided themselves into different branches. Races they call it. In one period, poor Earth, a completely power-crazy person nearly made a whole race extinct. Thus has the evil power swept through one time era after another.

Now I thought that you Earth, and I Nature, should bring about a change so that no humans or power-mad beings, either good or evil, can take part in making decisions. No, they must learn their smallness. They must learn to feel humility. Learn to appreciate both you, Mother Earth, and me, Nature. We have tried to turn a blind eye until now, but the moment has come when a turning point must happen.

Earth, open the chasm under the feet of the evil-natured beings, but preserve those who have done good. Open your prisons where many innocents are hidden. Enclose yourself quickly over their suffering Earth bodies, that they may come to a more beautiful kingdom and thereafter walk in a blissful world when the almighty one calls: 'Be!'

So can we both, you and I, help the almighty good power to make the Earth the humble and friendly planet it was meant to be from the beginning.

Beings will then experience their own powerlessness, learning that earthly riches and power are of no use. In their hour of need those high up in earthly power will ask and beg their slaves for help.

In their self inflicted desperation all thoughts on their so-called high heritage will evaporate as the darkness succumbs to the light. And Mother Earth, you and I will not get this for nothing. No! We have taken part and we see all the frightened and pained beings. Mother Earth, you who will swallow up many, you will feel these unhappy beings' desperate struggle. You will feel how your whole body will shake because of all the evil. You will become ill, but I, Nature, your friend, will help you to get well again. First you shall eject all the evil which you so obediently swallowed. Your whole inner being will come into uproar and the surviving beings will call this by different names: volcanic eruptions, earthquakes and floods. It will last for epochs, but you will regain your health and light, but be aware it will be very, very painful.

What will hurt most will be the inhuman pain that the living beings will experience. But Earth, you and I know that this is the completion of just eternal laws. Earth, you are now approaching a moment in the universe, in the eternal universe which doesn't know time. We, you and I, can mention time as long as we meet Earth dwellers. Soon I will call brother Storm. He will help you first and foremost to enclose the unjustly downtrodden in your arms. The storm will chase the sea over the land, the water will reach into its insides and help you to open your arms just at the right place and at the right time.

But we must be strong and not waiver until all crudeness and falsehood is eradicated from the planet. Beings will call out that this is a punishment which is going on all over the world. Oh, you Earth, how unknowing are these poor beings, surely there have been wise beings on the Earth, which told of the eternal justice and its laws. But haughtiness and greed for power have placed themselves before the speech of the wise. That is why it is necessary for this change. Mother Earth, be ready,

now comes the storm!

It looks like there's a storm brewing, said the haughty and proud queen, to her husband the king. Tell some of the servants to strengthen the poles round the old oak tree in the palace garden, so it will not be pulled up as the linden tree further down was, during the last storm. Also, tell all the servants, without exception, that they must be prepared to protect everything which belongs to us and our kingly palace.

The king looked out through the great palace window. He saw how large, grey-black storm clouds were gathering in the sky. He felt an inner anxiety which he couldn't explain. The king was a good fine person, who always wanted the good. But many times he had been driven by his power-hungry and cold queen to do things which had made him a shadow of his real human-I. The queen had been like an evil poison during her husband's whole time on Earth. She had caught him with her fine clothes and soft fine words. Words which were as empty and meaningless as a newly-made can which was ready to be filled with something good, but in the end all it had was a beautiful label.

Often he had asked the Almighty to take him away from this dreadful place. However, he couldn't just leave his position as the highest in the land, and say it was all the queen's fault. No, it's a good man who has the ability to like also what is less good.

The darkness grew deeper and deeper. The storm increased. Trees were thrown around like matchsticks and the houses in the castle garden lost their roofs. The hurricane increased. The large oak, the queen's favourite tree, swayed like rye in the wind. The lights from the castle swept over the park and the queen saw 'her oak' trembling as if in the throes of death.

A long time ago a little beggar woman had come to the castle. The queen now recalled every word this woman had said. She cannot remember why she had listened so carefully to this poor beggar, as she had a real distaste for poverty and people she regarded as worthless. But something the poor woman had said had caught her attention. Just tonight, in the terror of this evening when her proud oak was shaking in its inmost core, she remembered the woman's words.

'Don't think that a queen remains a queen forever. The justice of the Almighty doesn't work like that. Surely the Highest One has not meant it that some of us will always wander in the sunlit heights whereas others wander only in the shadows, in the valley. No, there will come a time when a great justice will come to the world. As a sign for this, you will one day see a large tree plucked out of the Earth by an invisible hand.' So said the poor woman, and off she went to continue her journey.

The queen had sometimes pondered on these strange words of the beggar woman, but she had also put them out of her mind. Surely, a great queen should not have to concern herself with what a little grey Earth rat has said.

But tonight, just when the storm was raging, both outside and in her innermost being, she sensed she could read the woman's words, as if they were written in fire before her.

The messages became more and more frequent. Many of the servants' quarters had been thrown to the ground. Terrified they came rushing to the castle. It seemed the only way to escape this stormridden night of terror. The king received them kindly. He invited them into the great hall, which was furthest away from the raging storm.

The queen's face was contorted in terror, but at the same time she was glowing red with rage over what she called the cowardice of the servants.

—Go out and care for our possessions, she said. This is what you are here for. Why should you be servants otherwise? The servants, looking like wounded animals, turned their pleading eyes to their king.

Out of his own free will and being a good man, the king would never have hurt anybody. He looked around. He saw his queen, she who had been his wife for many years. He saw the servants, men and women, he saw their children, the little ones he had known since they were born. He had seen them playing in the park and had played with them himself. He had known them as if they were his own children. He wasn't simply going to drive these people out on such a terrible night, just to satisfy the will of his power-hungry queen. No, never! As if a clear light began to shine, he saw past the storms and castles, past the servants and the queen, past even himself. He became conscious of something other than what could be grasped through earthly means.

—Stay in here and shelter from the power of Nature, said the king. Nobody will force you to go out on this terrible night. Let us have a little supper and eat together. Let us get the bedrooms ready for all of us, but first let's turn to the children.

The faces of the servants were filled with joy. This good man knew how to give joy and happiness to his fellow human beings. But the queen, did she feel any joy inside her?

No, her whole being was in uproar. She was about to silence her husband when a terrible crash was heard.

The oak, her own tree, had been pulled up by its hundred years old roots and was thrown against the castle.

After the fall of the oak there was a deathly silence. The only thing that could be heard was the ticking of the large clock. It was as if it came from another world.

The storm increased. The park was littered with fallen trees, roofs, fencing and anything that could be pulled loose.

The queen broke the silence.

—I demand that you servants go and do what you can to prevent more destruction.

—Don't you understand that we cannot stand against the power of Nature. So spoke the despairing king.

Within he felt something unpleasant taking shape. He felt himself overwhelmed by everything he had experienced since she had become his queen. All of her wickedness towards him and the servants. He felt a longing, deep in his inmost being, to see just an inch of humanity, humility and gratitude show itself in her.

In his utmost need he cried out for help. Forgetful of all the people around him, he prayed to the King of the World: Release me from this woman, take me where she cannot reach me with her hate and cunning. Do with me what you like, but let this evening be my last together with her.

Erect and silent he stood amongst his beloved servants and their children.

The king's words went forth from the room. They passed from servant to servant, from child to child, out into the free world, past the grey horizon and rose upwards, towards the light and to where he had called to for help.

The queen was immobile, like a lifeless statue, only her eyes were alive. They glowed with hate, humiliation and rage. She reached out a hand and pulled down a sword that was hanging on the wall.

Frozen with fear, the people were watching, completely unable to understand what was happening. With great power the queen pushed the sharp sword into the chest of the king. The storm was howling without, like an eternal accompaniment to the earthly drama taking place within.

But this was only an act towards the body of the king. His earthly dwelling had been killed, but his eternal 'I', his self and the self's 'I' returned to its true home: the king's dwelling place, called Eden.

Now he was able to look down on the Earth and see how sad everything was. He saw the Earth and the castle, the queen and the servants. He saw the little children. He saw the sword, which was half covered in red blood.

He also saw the castle park, destroyed and all the forces of Nature in uproar.

Where is everyone, the king was asking. Where is he, the Highest?

He could hardly think straight, as he had only just left the evil Earth.

The storm grew worse and worse. Some of the servants took up the body of the king and made a beautiful resting place in the king's own chamber.

Just as they were ready to show their beloved king their gratitude, the queen came and spoke words of hostility. She accused the servants of disobedience and told them that now she was in charge and that the king had had to pay with his life.

With hatred in his face, one of the servants stepped forward and spoke to the queen:

—Queen, your name is like the name of a viper. You are like a poisonous snake who has poisoned the life of our beloved king. You are false, dishonest, hungry for power and the strongest evidence of the power of evil. You have made nearly all our lives unbearable and if we hadn't had our beloved king, who himself was truth and goodness, we would never have been able to endure it. Now you are on your own! You have yourself killed the only person who has been good to you. He always defended you before us.

We cannot kill your earthly body, your king was never seeking for murder and for his sake we will let you go, you unworthy worm who is incapable of human feelings.

But we will imprison you, as we cannot help fearing for our lives. We will keep you imprisoned here in the castle until we know how it goes with the storm.

The bad weather raged over the Earth.

Only round the castle itself, Nature held its breath for some short minutes.

Now terror lived on the little planet which was called the Earth. Landmarks sank under the sea and new landmarks were raised up. The depths opened up under the people. Terror stricken, everyone rushed to seek shelter.

'What has happened', said the Earth dwellers. 'Is this the Day of Judgement the Bible spoke about?'

'Could this be the end for us Earth dwellers?' These things the people whispered and shouted alternately.

Round the earthly, kingly palace the storm increased in strength. A large extension to the palace had pulled away from the main building and crashed on to a beautiful statue called 'The Human Being', which was the most beautiful figure anyone had ever seen.

The statue was of a young, beautiful human being; of one who radiated beauty and goodness. The king had commissioned the statue from the world's greatest artist.

This was the artist who could form and shape everything with his hands. He had been the king's closest friend, and could see an angel living even in a block of marble.

Whilst the storm is raging and completing its work, this book will tell more about this artist. He was the artist who had decorated the whole of the king's palace with images of eternal beauty. The artist whose wisdom and power was able to transfer the highest eternal beauty and justice down here, to the lower planets. The artist who periodically came to the world of human beings, to bring them visions of eternal truth.

I shall now write down the poem that the good king wrote whilst he lived on the Earth. A poem that is about the artist who made the statue. The statue, which is the proof of the human beings' greatness and goodness. The statue which lies shattered by the work of Nature's awesome powers.

The King's Poem

Dedicated to my good friend, Carl Oskar,
who raised up the statue 'The Human Being'
in the Castle Park.

To my friend and brother, Carl Oskar

I shall now tell
about your other life
It comes from the heights
A voice who whispers
'write, write of the great artist
that mother Earth has brought forth,
write of the great work
which never can die'

The statue which you christened 'The Human Being'
shall adorn the Castle Park
It comes from the heights
It teaches truth and goodness

It reminds us human beings
of truth, cleanness, faith
Where the evil has taken root
'The Human Being' does not want to live

Not to live on the Earth
which has become an evil planet
Thereby the statue will return
into its own blissfulness
It will show the way
The way to unity on the Earth
The statue in wordless silence
The statue shattered by murder

If a murder has taken place
just here on this piece of land
Nature's own laws
will work in this park
A side wind shall topple
'The Human Being' of the artist
as a sign from the heights
that evil reigns here

I shall now tell
of another great beauty
that exists here on Earth

Of a dear friend and brother
A statue with the name 'David'
is made by his hand
A statue that adorns that place
is in another land

It is David and Goliath
you can behold in stone
You can see every expression
You can see every bone
David and Goliath
is not just a statue
No, these are living beings
They have their life from the heights

When you were born Carl Oskar
at a time and in a home
in a place that was Caprese
in the year fourteen hundred and seventy-five
your mother never knew
you were a great artist
for you were only six
when you were separated from her

Your mother left this Earth
so you were brought up by your father

and together with your brothers
who never understood you
Had no feeling for you
You with your artist's soul
And so you became for them
only a working slave

You felt the blood of the artist
which flowed within you
and you whispered so often
what is the meaning of this path
where I get only blows and scolding
when I paint, or draw
Who are these people
Who are my relations

And hard blows and scolding
became his daily toil
He who could never please his family
For whatever he said
and whatever he did
he received for it a blow
But the evil could not stop
the hope that lived within

His father was a hard man
who did not understand his son
and no one in the family
could be called good
For they were weak in their senses
And so his father thought
I will send this child to school
so he can learn how to behave

Then eventually it happened
When he had reached his thirteenth year
Then he was taught
by the brothers Ghirlandajo
But this only became a ridicule
as the boy already knew
that he within the kingdom of art
already was—a great prophet

One time, when the teacher
showed a whole female figure
the boy took his charcoal
and he began to work
to change the masterpiece
and hear how soon it was
that his schooling ended
but his marks were there anyway

Then his steps were turned
to Berfoldo, the stonecutter
and what happened next
you can find in his written story
As he started to cut
into the marble, hard and cold
he met Medici
who gave him all his love

Lorenzo di Medici
was the foremost man of Florence
and in the little boy
he found his best relative
Medici brought him to the castle
his new great friend
There the boy finally found
his first happy home

But everyone should know
that even so his life was hard
His mind contained a wisdom
which people couldn't understand
He didn't just make works of art
in stone and in churches
he also wrote sonnets
Seventy-one in all

So it happened at this time
that Pope Julius
was building his new temple
A house of beauty for the Lord
But the Pope was haughty
and proud in his breast
and soon everyone could hear
the proud voice of the Pope

Send for Michaelangelo
Ask him to come here
He shall honour the Pope
and paint a suite full of beauty
A suite that will belong to the world
when I have left this Earth
So spoke this proud Pope
in these famous words

But the artist, like the Pope
also had his temperament
And this friendship was often
more than just a joke
And Miche you should know
was independent
and made up his mind about this interior
without the answer of the Pope

Then the ceiling would be decorated
in the dark Sistine Chapel
It was so dark in there
like a constant dark night
where only a few shutters
let in the light
Hear what has been said
about this temple house

Under the ceiling of this building
a structure of poles was made
and there lay the great artist
painting these holy images
Now hear what he painted
Our artist wise and knowing
Yes, the Creation and the Flood
from the first book of Moses

First we see the Almighty Father
with his finger stretching forth
He touches the man's head
whose name is Adam, the Son
created in the image of the Lord
though a human he is,
and through Eternity
he will teach about the worlds

We even see Eve
sheltering in the Lord's arm
She is so beautiful to behold
her gaze is human and warm
The images are alive
as the artist gave them life
as everything that Miche painted
comes wholly down from Heaven

Then statues of Moses were created
for the Funeral Monument
And even this art is from the heights
Moses is so alive
Holy wrath within his gaze
And it has been said
you can sometimes hear Moses
murmuring his words

One could write volumes about this
About the great Michaelangelo
about his great message
about his wise faith
The art he left behind
is art without measure,
it is given by the Lord,
given to the people

We will now wander further
A couple of Earth years on
We wander to the graves
where the Medici men lie
We gaze at the statues
two proud noble men
amongst whom Michaelangelo
had his greatest friends

One is Giuliano,
the other Lorenzo
They have life in their gaze
and they live in the church
And just in this room
the artist has drawn himself
next to the proud monuments
under the vault within the church

But still the burden
was not yet over for the artist
Also another wall shall be adorned
of the Sistine Chapel
There in seven years he painted
the work of the Last Judgement
on the wall in the Chapel
in the holy space, the Sistine Chapel

There you can gaze
on the open graves
There stand the wretched dead
What will be their sentence?
But innermost in their hearts
the artist has hidden the secret
He has found the answer
that life is for eternity

But still many a task
lies before the great artist
To complete St Peter's Church
and its beauty is still there
He said: I am now an old man
soon to be fetched by death
It was in February
he left the earthly plane

He wrote a testament
of three distinct reasons
On top of the first page
it reads: take my soul
O Lord, and keep it
from the evil, false murder
On the second line
one reads these words

Now, mother, take the body
and embrace it in your arms
I have asked the good Father
to take my soul ashore
and all my belongings
my relatives and friends can have
I cannot take them with me
into Heaven

Now the earthly life is ended
of the man sent from God
Year fifteen hundred and sixty-four
He had this message from an angel
Now you have completed
what God demanded from you
So whispered the angel
from the highest sphere

But everyone is born again
so our God has decided
and thirteen years thereafter
the door stood ajar again
it was time for the artist
again to come to Earth
also in this life
he is anointed artist

Peter Paul Reubens
sees the light of day
this time in Germany
In Siegen stood his house
and living in exile
his father sentenced for a crime
they fled to Antwerp
just where they had lived before

Even in this life
he became a great artist
who through his beautiful paintings
teaches the world of beauty
He only stayed in the spiritual world
for thirteen Earth years
He didn't think he had finished
therefore he returned again

He painted like the last time
paintings, ceilings, walls
he painted in the courts
he painted in the chambers
he painted all the beauty
of humans, flowers, animals
his art possessed life
and the world wondered how he did it

But no one on the Earth
knew at all
that Michaelangelo and Reubens
were the same person
Even though they saw
their art was related to one another
But the answer to the riddle
no one found out

It is a grace from God
to behold past lives
Sometimes on the Earth it happens
when the Lord says 'Be'
Then someone on the Earth
can see it with clear sight
and will tell
about the vision

But messages will not come
until the senses are awake
On the Earth there aren't many
who know the true message
that human beings are born again
Not many comprehend
But simple are the laws
that all will come again

The smallest little flower
constantly reappears
Human beings are born again
though that is difficult to comprehend
Christ has spread
just these words of truth
That's why he was crucified
as people wanted murder

To slaughter the Son of God
who brought all truth
To help the people escape
the anguish of lies
But human beings were shallow
Tight in their chests
It was difficult for them
to listen to the true voice of Christ

The time when Christ said
do not weep
my dear ones
I will declare
that everyone will come again
An earthly life is just a second
in the life of eternity
We are constantly born again
when the Lord says—'Be'

A small group of people
found the truth
in his message
All the others said
He is not sent from God
This cannot be the truth
that all are born again
We think he has come
with words from the Devil

So spoke the people
from Christ's time on Earth
Many were the doubters
who with the faithful fought
Now again God's truth
reaches to the human world
and it will reach everyone
The ignorant and the wise

I will write books
so the Lord has said
until all the great truths
from round the world are known
then all people shall know
that they come again
I will write the message of the Lord
till all will understand

Comprehend they lived before
and constantly are born again
That life is partly Earth
and partly of heaven
We meet old friends
our brothers, sisters, mother and father
Life is graceful
and God's love eternally great

Humans then shall know
that everything will come again
That what you do against your foe
What you do against your friend
forms your own life
So are the eternal laws
which the Lord of the heights
proclaims forever—'Become'

Here ends the poetry of the king. The poem he wrote for his good friend, the one who created the statue 'The Human Being'. 'The Human Being' which lay shattered in the park.

We now turn from the world of poetry to cold reality.

The reality of planet Earth. What has happened since we last visited the castle?

This is what this book will tell.

A great silence rested over humanity's Earth, a silence so frightening and so hideous, so immense, it was almost unbearable.

Now we return to the castle park. What are we met by? Yes, by death, by cold, by chaos, suffering and darkness—a world without life. The park looks like a battleground left from a cruel war. The castle is demolished. It looks like a heap of stones thrown by a giant. Only a few forlorn bird-cries break the silence.

Nature holds its breath and beholds its work. Now I've done my part, Earth, the eternal voice of Nature is heard

to say. Now remains your work! You, Earth, don't hesi-
tate, go on, it's time for your part of the agreement.

The Earth, sad and confused, witnessing the wild
witch dance of Nature, did not feel like continuing this
dance of death.

But a promise is a promise.

Where shall I start? wondered the Earth.

Nature came immediately to her aid.

Start in the castle park. Under the ruins lies the good
king's queen, imprisoned by the servants, but there is
still a chance she will escape.

You, Earth, open your deepest abyss right there under
the room where she lies. Hide and imprison her in the
hot core of your being. She will experience how the
eternal laws of justice work. If the evil queen had not put
the sword into the good king's side she wouldn't have
been imprisoned, but she created her own punishment.

Afterwards, open up to those like her. Close yourself
over them, so that they will no longer poison the Earth
for the foreseeable future.

So, the time is at hand to help those poor and pained
beings. Those who live in the prisons and torture camps,
who suffer in all the rooms of hospitals wherever they are.

But, Earth, don't forget to act quickly so those already
pained shall not have suffered in vain.

And remember, O Earth, to call down the angels from

the heights, that they may fetch the suppressed, pained souls.

The bodies you may take care of as you please. Don't worry, all those you trapped inside you will have their new bodies when the time comes. But, Earth, there is an exception. The queen! You must keep her for only a while. Even for her this imprisonment is not forever although that would seem fair. You will not keep her and her henchmen forever.

Her king, who was as good as the queen was evil, was careful over the laws of the kingdom. He never judged anyone harshly. Now the king is in Heaven and looks down on the chaos of the Earth. He sees his imprisoned queen, sees into her wormlike soul and the falsehood as he remembers it. Not the slightest iota of pardon or regret rose up from her.

At one point the king said to her: 'Don't forget, my queen, whatever you say and whatever you do, I am always prepared for reconciliation if in humbleness and in your need you will turn towards me.'

But her heart was hard and cruel. In the end she relied on the help of her servants, a few of whom always did what she said. But where were they now? Would they soften when they saw their diamond-bestudded queen, imprisoned under this mass of earth?

But these servants, who had blindly followed the

queen's will, were also buried within the Earth's deathly grip.

The Earth, soft and good if no one disturbs her, but firm and fair in her senses, now began the completion of their combined response.

–Lend me a little of your power, O Nature, said the Earth. Let the seas wash over my bloodstained body, let the ocean's purity take away the poison and rottenness which has had its dwelling on me. In this way you can help me to open the depths. Nature, I am ready.

Again, Nature let loose her power. The storm pressed its masses of water on to the sick and wounded Earth. Every valley and crack was filled with water. The Earth shook and roared deep in its innermost being. Its hot intestines were thrown up in glowing cascades and the abyss was opened, swallowing mercilessly anything which lived.

The large beautiful cities with all their magnificent buildings were razed to the ground. Only gaping holes were left in their place. Forests, mountains, valleys, palaces, dwelling houses, parks, roads, everything sank into the depths. People, animals, plants, yes, everything that was on the Earth was swept away. But still there were landmarks and some living creatures left.

The choirs and beings of the Heavens followed the drama on the Earth. The good king sat on a beautiful throne. His mind was heavy with sorrow, sorrow over all the evil that existed on the Earth—the Earth which from the beginning had been a dwelling place for goodness. The Earth which the king had intended as a kingdom for himself and his queen.

From the throne of the king, where his servants also were, a song resounded.

It was a song of praise sung by the king's servants, both great and small.

And from the depths came the voices of the faithful servants who were still there inside the Earth.

'We must rejoice and be happy as our king is back in the Heavens above us, and everyone in our universe shall honour and obey him.'

And behold, a beautiful shining white horse was seen next to the throne and on the horse 'The Human Being', which was the statue from the king's park. On his head he had a crown of heavenly stars and his gaze was as clear as a well's fresh water. He was clothed in a blood-red mantle.

This beautiful man on the white horse spoke, and said:

> *I went to the Earth where human beings live*
> *but only in an image-form*
> *I should stop the murders*
> *so the king had said*
> *I was shaped by the hands*
> *of a holy, great artist*
> *I was spoken of in many countries*
> *so people could learn the truth*
>
> *I stood in a herb garden*
> *with the king and queen*
> *I should take care*
> *of the old and young*
> *As a symbol of love*
> *I came to the king's castle*
> *but reached by the law of Nature*
> *I had to return from where I came*

I was smashed to the ground
by earthly laws
So in the kingly park
'The Human Being' was murdered
My message, in shreds
stayed on the Earth
Not even the priest
could stop the murder

I returned to the Father
who gave me his crown
Now, my servants there in your rows
I ask you in all humbleness
to think good things of your neighbours
give your hand to the sinner
I want to give you the best
I give you this kingly land

A land where we shall live
in blissful peace
Where no one will be lost
Where no one will know strife
and the evil power
is bound deep
in the grey abyss
Now I will give you the answer

But everyone should know
this is a time of trial
we don't know the outcome
still there is war and strife
The evil powers fought
to tear away its fetters
though the peaceful time
dampened the evil raging cries

A world, we shall see
pure like a clear well
Only unity shall reign
That is the promise of my Father
Where everyone shall live as friends
and evil is forgotten
Where all will know each other
and all anxiety will be hidden

I live by your side
I, the king of kings
No one will suffer
not young or old
and all the fields will be flowering
and the sky will shine clear blue
but rain will also fall
so you can understand

Constant sunshine is tireing
even for the greatest king
Not yet everyone knows
that even joy can be heavy
So my dear ones
everything is changing
so everything can be bearable
both the rain and the blue sky

The 'old ones' wrote texts
on eternal paradise
They also wrote old books
about the price of evil
that all evil souls
will fall into the red sea of Satan
where even the smallest flower
lies in a grave of death

The 'old ones' also wrote
that Satan gains his freedom
when the time of grace is past
That is not the law
which has been
as it were from eternity
No one can be forced
to remain in eternal blissfulness

Neither to Hell
people shall forever go
They don't know my Father
if they think that is what he intended
How would my Father
be in his heart
if standing in the abyss
he would judge the sinners

No, they themselves have built
dwellings of both good and bad
they always will be forgiven
Tell me, do you understand?
You yourself write the words
in the great book of life
let your life on Earth
guide you to walk wisely

Be good towards your neighbour
live well and justly
always do your best,
that is my only request
We are together
We will be given a kingdom
I know, my friends
that you have understood

My Father wrote the laws of All
it will last until eternity
if everything pleases him
then nothing will fall
See the flowers in Nature
they follow the call of the All
look also at the animals
how they obey our God

You humans are the greatest
in this All-encompassing great world
and you shall also be
the first that knows through me
you all will 'reign' with me
in a thousand years
and if there shall be more
you must decide yourself

Because no one can decide
over another one's soul
as that would squash
my Father's law of freedom
God will not inflict any pain
not even on the greatest sinner
He does not have such low thoughts
that is only what humans think

Behind the white horse and the rider in the red mantle came many other riders. All were riding white horses, but these other riders were dressed in white mantles. Only the first rider's mantle was red.

The king stepped forward and said:

Look, this beautiful man is my son. When he visited the Earth no one cared about his greatness. 'Hail, my son, you will inherit the crown and my kingdom.'

There shall be a new kingdom at a set time. Only goodness will rule and all the evil of this universe will be bound together. All those who have not done wrong will reign with him.

He will not wear the same clothes as the other riders. No, the red mantle he wears is proof of the human blood that ran out of his body on to the Earth. The blood ran out to the last drop, so that only a lifeless statue was left.

And now my son shall become King and he will rule forever over this universe. You who are gathered will know it.

I, the king, will seek for my fallen queen when her imprisonment comes to an end. But everyone shall have their free will, even the queen. That's why nothing is evident yet. Even I, the King, follow the laws of Nature, as do the Son and the queen.

I go to the worlds above this kingdom, I leave my kingly crown, as earthly kings do for their sons. What I will then accomplish is not for your ears or understanding. The time will come though when everyone shall know the truth.

My son, who is the king from now on, will give you all the answers. He is completely free to rule his universe according to his own sense and mind. He has now reached completeness. He is the Lord. But he is not a powerful and terrifying God. No, he is the God who has loving thoughts. He is also the God's God and the Lord's Lord.

But the evil in the universe is not extinguished, as yet. There will always exist struggles of one kind or another. But there will always be moments of calm. There will be a balancing between the powers: the powers that control all life of the universe. It was never the intention that one of them should overpower another. This is what I say, as the king who reaches into a higher space. The space above this kingdom's universe. The space that no human being knows. There are no limits, floors or ceilings for the highest Lord.

The Lord is the greatest judge. Everyone, without exception, who writes or says anything that goes against this, writes and speaks untruth.

I, the Son of the lord, born into the human world, but who existed in my Father's kingdom long before the world was created, have spoken to you, who so far are humans. But I say to you, it will not rest with this, everything goes along in eternal tracks. I have stood where human beings stand. I have already told you that I was born into the world as an ordinary person. Everyone will stand where I stand. I am descended from the house of David and this is the truth.

You shall return in earthly body, a body of flesh, blood, bones, sinews and everything that is needed for the soul to live an earthly life. But this body shall not be plagued by illness or any other evil, and no souls can lead these bodies to do evil.

Everyone stood still and listened in silence to the King.

The newly crowned King looked with immeasurable love at the crowd.

—My friends, speak, speak, He said and stretched forth his arm as if He wanted to embrace them all.

The beautiful flock looked at their Master and Lord with super-earthly joy in their gaze.

A man from the first line stepped forward and said:

—Master, our joy makes us speechless, but I have to use words, for just as Nature writes down all its eternal laws so also it needs small words to be able to speak of earthly beings.

Master, the greatest joy for this flock is your joyous message that not a single being will be lost forever. Oh, great Master, have not uncountable beings throughout time been frightened to death by the threat of eternal hell. Also we, your flock, got the wrong idea about life on the other side of the world. How often, Lord, did I not think of the Bible's message and those very thoughts, which are read in the worldly churches. How could a single being go into eternal bliss knowing that so many would go into eternal hell? Lord, I never had an answer to my constant recurring questions; the Bible became in many parts a mysterious secret.

Now, when everything lies open for us, Lord, I would like, together with this large gathering, to help you to proclaim these simple truths. Truths that everyone without exception reaches the light and goodness. And so it is we, Lord, who have come a little further on the road, who can help our fellow travellers.

The flock came forward, one after the other, and spoke.

—Lord, where is the kingdom where we will reign together with you?

We have seen the human Earth. We have seen it naked, wounded, bloody, bare. Evil, sick vapours rise from its depths. Surely, we cannot find a kingdom of goodness there.

Those who wanted evil have not yet left their dead earthly corpses. The wrathful queen lies under the ruins of the castle.

Where shall we find our kingdom?

One after another the heavenly flock spoke. The King of Heaven and Earth smiled and silently, humbly and with great love he listened to all their questions.

—My dears, said the king, encompassed by his Mantle of

Life. Even though you all know this truth in your hearts, you are still confused by this new knowledge of earthly life. Up to now it has been obvious to you that my Father has never punished anyone. Everyone should know that my Father as well as I are completely free of all thoughts of revenge. I have previously said that the law that applies to how each one lives is: 'as human beings sow, so shall they reap'. Those who sow wheat will reap wheat; those who sow weeds will reap weeds. Also, those who sow love will reap love, and those who sow sorrow will reap sorrow.

But don't forget that free will never ceases.

Now my dears, perhaps you wonder where the kingdom is? Come, my dears, and I will show you a performance which comes from the Earth. It is not a performance where we will clap our hands and be happy. It is not a play where somebody says lines which they have memorized. No, it is a terrible reality. A reality which the Earth dwellers have created for themselves out of their free will.

Evil is not yet uprooted from planet Earth. There are still some evil thinking souls who want to take the power of the universe away from my Father.

Human beings have in many ways reached so far in their earthly development that they can reach out into the universe, to other heavenly spheres. As long as it happens in the name of peace and the desire to know, nothing dangerous will happen. Some beings have had to pay for their adventure by losing their earthly bodies. But this was not sin. The adventure seekers were following the wishes of their country. The country was large and occupied a large part of the Earth.

But there are many countries on this planet Earth.

Now, my friends, you will see a drama which will always remain as a wound to your senses.

I read your thoughts: Our King and Master, how can you let us experience this? When we saw how large parts of the Earth opened and swallowed up everything around it, that was enough.

—But now I say to you, this is necessary for the future. Good and evil will always fight against each other and sometimes goodness gets the upper hand and sometimes evil. That is a fundamental law which can never be taken away.

You mustn't misunderstand me and think: What shall we fight for then, if we cannot eradicate evil?

I can translate evil and say instead 'negative force' and translate goodness and say 'a positive force'. It is both these forces which are always active.

It is the fundamental meaning of the law that they act normally. With normality there must always be a certain resistance. A negative resistance.

But it mustn't become so great that even a single being will suffer. It shall only be so large so that everything is held in its given place in the universe. It is right and true that even the present evil queen seeks to find her way back to her positive side, the good king.

Everything is constantly pulsating and in this state the universe exists in the way the High Almighty has planned it, when everything pulsates with these immeasurable forces, but in each pulse beat all that there is is present.

When these things melt together and become a united force and come into harmony, then the whole mighty universe is filled with joy, song, health, laughter, bird-song; it becomes a cloudfree heaven, there is good food, good drink, nice kind people wherever one looks, the animals are tame, the winds calm, no one raises their voice, everything breathes of a super-earthly peace.

But listen now, little Earth children, not a single being in the whole complete universe can stand this eternal peace. Not one I say. Not even my Father, who is the highest I know. What he has above himself or beneath him no one knows. Maybe he has unaccountable kings above himself, maybe he alone is the sovereign ruler. It doesn't concern a single being that is beneath him.

No servant has a right to demand a reckoning from his Lord. Just as little as I demand from my Father, just as little shall you my friends demand a reckoning from me.

My Father, who has gone to greater and different tasks has left this universe to me. And see, I am your God and King.

I said before that the negative force and the positive force shall pulsate according to the Supreme Law. What do I mean? I read this in your questioning thoughts.

Listen carefully, and hide it in your senses. Just this selected flock, which also many of the prophets have spoken about, shall take this message further to the beings of the world. Nature and Life in the universe is much wider and bigger than any soul dressed in an earthly body can comprehend. That's why I use the opportunity to tell you this, while your souls are free of your narrow costume.

When the negative force reaches into the positive, then everything is like the golden city. Everything is gleaming and shining; blue skies are everywhere, sun shining and songs of praise are sung to the Lord of All. Just sometimes, the meaning of the archetypal law will show that the forces cancel themselves and become independent of each other.

There will come cloudy days, rain, overcast, songs will recede, like the birds who don't want to sing on a cloudy day.

Beings feel they need to make an effort to re-establish balance in the universe.

All created beings have these two forces within themselves and they should all comprehend that each can create the kingdom they want to live in. It is exactly this which is paradise.

I feel in my innermost soul that you are waiting impatiently for the dramatic end of the Earth. But be prepared, because human eyes have never seen such devastation.

The flock gathered around its King and Master, at the outermost border of 'heaven'. The heaven which has nothing to do with the earthly vault of heaven.

Was there anybody left alive on the Earth after the terrible storm?

Yes, the Earth had not managed to swallow everyone. It was as if the Earth was full up inside.

In stillness the King and the whole group looked down upon the earth.

The King spoke before the drama of death began.

–You know that atoms exist in the service of beings. Atoms are used for destruction and death, like nuclear weapons. Look carefully, my friends, how the beings (who are still alive on the Earth) behave.

Look at all the machines they fly, their spaceships or flying machines which they use to reach other planets.

As long as human beings believed in the help of the Almighty Father and only in an adventurous spirit in the service of peace, they travelled to outlying planets and nothing dangerous happened.

But see, my friends, though I have to ask your pardon for my sad tears which will run down my face.

—See those fire-spraying space rockets which are fired from the big land which for a long time had been inferior to that other country, that had visited the Moon planet in curiosity but peacefulness. Now they have taken a nuclear weapon which they will explode on the grey, bare, crater-bedecked surface of the Moon.

Be prepared and see how the poor planet is shook to its core after this nuclear bomb. As there is no atmosphere which can make a protective sheath, there will be a chain-reaction explosion round the planet. See there how the ship that brings death has already left and finds safe ground to land, back on the Earth.

—But, my dears. Nature is a stern, as well as a fair Master. The beings of the Earth have stepped over the holiest of holies of all Nature's laws.

Sad and hard-pressed Nature speaks to the Earth, pointing to the fatally attacked Moon and says:

—You Earth, after the death of the Moon, will only survive for a matter of hours. Earth, with my help you will swallow up the rest of life, all the volcanoes will rise up and light your wounded body. You will have a holy cremation. But your soul, good Earth, will get a new sheath. You will also get a new guardian who will restore order in all and everything. The Lord will split a large planet and provide the core for a new Earth; the small part of it shall be the guardian or the new Moon.

Exactly as it is at this moment for you, O Earth, so shall it become. The Moon is a part of your body, which the Father put there to be your Moon, as otherwise no living creature could have lived on you.

Now had Nature spoken again to the Earth.

At the heaven's edge the crowd saw how the whole Earth opened itself up to become one sea of fire. They saw how the spaceships circled over the glowing abysmal planet, they saw how the Moon now burnt like a blood-red sea, the friend and guardian of the Earth split into innumerable parts. Red glowing pieces shattered throughout the dark vastness of space.

The Earth, the Moon's 'mother', met the same fate and with this anguish of death in their senses, the spaceships circled in her empty universe. No Earth, no Moon, no heaven. Nothing, only empty nothingness.

Their cry of anguish could not reach beyond the spaceships. The crowd saw how the expensively built spaceship dived into the glowing Earthly abyss. The spaceship, which would have given the power-lustful masters on the Earth new planets and worlds where they would rule over the rest of the inhabitants, was destroyed.

But the Lord Father wants to decide the order of everything Himself. Now the Earthly beings had gone far enough, as far as he would allow it.

Now were heard immeasurable calls of complaint, screams from the abyss, which pierced space like spearheads. There was the smell of burnt forest, burnt flesh, smoke and an impenetrable fog settled over the dying Earth.

See the steaming Earth splintering into a million pieces. The Earth which for a long time had been the dwelling place of people.

Then an ear-deafening din was heard. Without border, without measure, without comparison. Like a giant fire display, the Earth was shattered. After that terrible moment everything became black—an impenetrable darkness.

Gone was the Earth, gone the Moon. Empty was the space outside the 'land' where they now stood.

But where is the kingdom, Master, the kingdom where we will live with you? questioned the crowd with sadness.

The Master in his red mantle answered: My beloved, my friends, the Lord Father has promised you a new heaven and Earth. Behold, you will soon see the most wondrous thing. Behold your new kingdom. See how fine the new Earth gleams in all its splendour. See her guardian, the new Moon. See heaven. Never before has a more beautiful heaven been seen, transparent blue, with a colour so clear, so mild, reminiscent of the Lord Father's eternal gaze. See the mountains, forests, valleys, fields and the flowers. See also the guardian, the follower, who will help you establish a new kingdom.

The faithful flock, who through their continuous loving wandering in the universe, will live with the Lord Master at the appointed time, gazed out over space and saw with deep humbleness and gratitude, the new heaven and the new Earth.

But their joy was not complete.

–Tell us, King, what has happened to the poor ones, down there in the depths. We cannot feel such joy at this moment when so many are suffering.

The Lord replied: Don't be sad, my precious friends, when the time is right you will help these poor beings towards light and peace. Then you shall tell them the only truth: that love forgives everything, knows everything and can do everything.

Tell them they have not been condemned to eternal hell, just as little as they have been granted eternal heaven or paradise. Tell them that beings shape their own kingdoms. Tell them that free will really is better to be used for the good than the bad.

And remember, my dears, that it has been your humbleness and love that led you here to this kingdom of bliss. I can also call it the kingdom of experiment, where human beings can feel what it is like to live in unity and love with all creatures.

I can tell you that these wretched beings who committed evil shall, step by step, creep towards the light. I cry within me when I think how loudly and without a quiver in their voice the mighty men of the church talk about my Lord Father's immense wrath. Preaching that he sends all his fallen children into eternal damnation.

I have so often seen these frightened people, carrying in their inner vision a vista of eternal fire, which is to make them suffer into eternity. Human beings who think like this within themselves live in such a way that they think they will never reach the kingdom of bliss.

Now, my dears, after a thousand-year kingdom you will, without exception, be placed in different parts of the world where those wretched beings will begin to wander towards the light. Nothing is given for nothing. I, your Helper and King, will not demand this of you. No, by your own free will you can go to these wretched and weak ones who have followed the path of evil.

It is an unwritten law for the souls of those who think

rightly that they should always help the oppressed and weak on the road to eternity.

Now the time is at hand that we shall take command of the kingdom (the time which is not counted, but always has to be counted when one speaks about an earthly life).

I will be with you constantly during your wandering on the Earth, in thought, word and deed.

I hear your silent question, how will you be born there? It is such a clean fine planet where evil has not yet visited. Shall you arrive there like newly born human children, or shall you arrive like grown-up Earth dwellers?

As yet you cannot freely look forwards for yourselves or backwards into eternity; it is also not that everything will be decided at the same time. I, your King and Master, can see the past and see through the fog and sheath which protects both the old and the new eternity. I speak mainly about eternity, since the concept of time belongs to the circling planets and the beings on the planets.

Now, you will get to know how you shall build and live in this peaceful kingdom. There are no inhabitants until we get there. I say we, for I, your Master and King, will also be there. As I am the Lord, all knowing, almighty and all wise, I can in a Godlike fashion 'plant' the inhabitants on the Earth who are worthy to receive your earthly bodies.

How this will happen I will keep to myself for the time being, as it is easy to mock miracles.

What I say now is written in books which are read in the human world. That's why I have to be very careful that everything which is given to the present inhabitants on Earth is either told in parables, stories or other ways, so that those with seeing eyes will see and those with hearing ears will hear.

Now, my beloved friends, we will go and rest before we commence our thousand years of wandering. A wandering which is a way into higher worlds.

There are many on the Earth in this eternal moment who will read what is here written and say:

This is against the Bible. We do not believe in such tales.

I say to them, large parts of the Bible go against my Father, the Lord and my words. Everything is forever changing, but God's great eternal law of love is unchangeable. Rest 'awhile', my dears, we will meet again in the kingdom of goodness.

—Have you read the book of the wise man from the valley?

A young woman asked this question of her friend.

—No, answered her friend, but what is it about?

—If you listen to me I shall gladly tell you. He speaks about an evil Earth which was here before our Earth was populated in this place in the universe. He also writes of a little planet which followed the Earth or was placed next to it. There were beings there who only wanted to do bad things to each other, took each other's possessions, fought about power, about glory and the kingdom of the Earth. At last they fought on the little planet which they called the Moon. But that wasn't enough. They took each other's lives.

So, when the evil became too great, they exploded both their own planet as well as the Moon, so there was only chaos, darkness, death and pain.

The old Earth and the old Moon became a fine, fine dust, which whirled hither and thither in the universe, just like the death-bringing rocket-men who were floundering in a desolate and empty space after they had spread the evil poison: the 'nuclear weapon', queen Lucifia's own poison.

So, our world came into space where Earth and Moon had been before the split.

We often wonder about the grey ring around our planet. The wise man tells us about this in his book of wisdom.

It is the split-up Earth and Moon who long to become a whole and totally healthy planet again. The exploded dust was pulled here, where they had lived before as whole planets.

But our planet, the good 'Prisma', could, through this kingdom's light, keep the evil particles at a distance. Then they formed a belt like a ring around our whole planet. It is the shadow of this ring that we constantly see on our planet.

The wise man also writes in his book that just such a ring around a planet is proof that an evil planet, which existed before in the same place in space, was once split.

Such are the holy laws of the Lord, the great King, who can let things remain whole or split according to His eternal laws.

Sometime in eternity all these particles will again gather into one body and find a place in the universe.

Then the atoms will have become cleansed through the long ring dance around the good planets, which form a kind of kernel.

The good young woman on the good planet Prisma has ceased to speak. For her, death and war are incomprehensible. She lives in peaceful times, she remembers hardly anything about the talks she and others had with the Highest Master before this Earth life. She only knows that this world is one of light and is beautiful. She knows that she can trust her fellow men, and that she is free from illness and pain, needs and misery. She knows that she lives in a beautiful paradise; she also knows that it is a reward for the good people.

But she knows more through the old wise man's book. She knows that evil can gain entry to this planet. She knows that the stay on the planet Prisma is determined by time. The great shadow, which the evil Earth dust ring throws, will continually remind the inhabitants of the planet of the other large power which also rules in the universe. This shadow shall continue to be the help to escape darkness and the unknown. The coldness in the nearness of the shadow is icy cold. Like a foreign world the unfriendly black belt lies around the planet as if holding it in an iron grip.

After reading the wise man's book, she now views the world in a different light. Now she has awakened to the tiptoeing of enemies, enemies whose jealousy, irritation, meanness and other signs represent the spirit of the evil queen.

But who is the wise man? It is said that he lived on the other Earth. He said that he already knew the great laws of truth.

At the end of the wise book, which he calls 'The Eternal Spring', he tells how the evil people beheaded him. A woman belonging to the abyss demanded his head on a plate. He remembers the ghastly Earth.

Because of that, he wrote the book of wisdom.

The Earth had been a good planet. Just like Prisma. But the evil powers took the Earth into its grip. Just as they could begin to see traces of unrest and unfriendliness here on Prisma. But 'The Eternal Spring' tells of all the demons of the Earth which came hunting over the wounded Earth planet. It tells of the terror which the humans on the Earth felt when it rebelled against the evil. It tells of all the laws of Nature, how everything has its eternal track, how all beings with their free will can lead the world either towards joy or sorrow, life or death, war or peace.

With his book, 'The Eternal Spring', the wise man wanted to tell about the mystic black shadow, the memory from the evil Earth, the planet that became dust because hate and evil lived in the universe.

It is the planet which the wise man had seen bursting into pieces, and the Moon he saw becoming blood after the nuclear explosion. He also saw mountains sink and valleys fill with roaring masses of water, houses and homes buried in the Earth, human beings killed and disfigured, children and grown ups, all races, crying in anguish and despair in the face of all this death and destruction. Human beings, animals and plants were held in the grip of death.

Once there was an evil tale told about the human kingdom–*when the storm came.*

Written by me, Barbro Karlén
1969

A MOMENT IN THE
BLOSSOM KINGDOM

Only those
who want
to follow me to the Blossom Kingdom
should read what I'm writing,
those who are not interested
will anyway think it is childish.
I am childish and I like it,
I don't know what it feels like
to be grown up.
Maybe I will never be an adult.
Those who want to go
on the journey to the Blossom Kingdom
should assemble here.
You are all welcome.
Now we depart.

The Journey to the Blossom Kingdom

So, we who are going have now met. This is not an ordinary journey where you have to bother with passport, money and travelling clothes, or a vaccination because there may be illnesses. No, nothing is needed by the traveller—not even clothes!

When you read about it, at first many will think that the passengers are those we call the dead.

They aren't. They are ordinary living earth people.

Earth people who have stood the test which means that they can endure the journey. Astronauts also get tested to see who can endure.

Somebody says, 'You said everyone can come, so a test shouldn't be needed.'

No it isn't, those who wish to go have passed the test. In them is a longing to experience something which doesn't exist on the earth. Maybe you wonder how I can know of the Blossom Kingdom? Well, I shall tell you!

The Blossom Kingdom's own wonderful Blossom

Goddess came flying to me on a clear moonlit night and told me the tale of her kingdom.

I was the most childish person she had seen on the earth and that's why she told me the tale. I made a journey with her; therefore I know the way and now I want to make the journey with those who wish to come.

Now the journey starts. The night is still and clear. The heavens are covered with sparkling stars. You don't need to bring anything on the journey. You go as naked as when you were born. You get clothes from the Blossom Kingdom when you get there.

We don't fly. We reach there through our thoughts. The journey goes fast, past a million worlds. It is too fast to grasp and the light gets brighter and brighter. The Blossom Kingdom is so far away that we have to think beyond our own Sun.

I have been quiet the whole time, but the closer we get the more curious I get. I am only an ordinary childish earthling.

—Blossom Goddess, are we going to see another Sun in your kingdom?

—No, she says immediately. We don't need any help from a Sun.

—Won't we be cold? I did not even bring any clothes.

—No, little frozen earth child, you will not freeze. The

Blossom Kingdom is its own Sun, Moon and Stars. It has within and without all that it needs.

Remember, little earth child, the more curious you are, the more you can believe in, the more you can perceive and hear.

We were getting closer and closer. I was naked when the journey began, now I was more than naked. I sensed that I didn't need to speak to the Blossom Goddess, as she knew my thoughts before they turned to words. I also didn't need to listen. I saw or maybe I felt her words, and her answers.

Suddenly, we arrived at the uncomparably beautiful planet. I looked at myself. My body, or rather my being, had transparent clothes that resembled the most beautiful flowers. They changed colour according to what I thought. I looked around. Many had come to welcome me. The colour of their beings was far more beautiful than mine. Mine changed to dirty grey, grey black, black or just white. All the others had such beautiful colours, indescribable if you haven't seen them. The good Blossom Goddess was my constant companion and knew what I was thinking.

She said:

–Little earth child, no one can give you colours for your clothes, it can only come from your inner self. As you have just left the earth you still think egoistically and have selfish thoughts. You are mostly interested in yourself.

—No, I protested, it's not like that.

My clothes turned darker and darker. What should I do?

—Come with us to the blossom temple where you can pray to the Highest Divinity. His name is Blossom Father and He knows everything. He is everything. He sees everything. He helps us, as He is the helper that was, is and will be forever.

Yes, yes. My clothes coloured by my thoughts got lighter bit by bit. It felt as if I were having a cool bath on a hot summer day.

We arrived at the blossom temple. The whole temple looked like a flower. The temple bells were formed like lilies of the valley and the sound was mild and clear like a gentle forest breeze. In the beautiful temple hall there were flower angels in beautiful pictures and music came from every flower; the stillness was complete. The Blossom Kingdom's highest Blossom Father entered. He gave what all earth people really want, which is absolute faith. This is the highest faith, higher than everything.

I turned to the Blossom Goddess. She already knew my silent question.

—What about Christ? Our Christ whom Christians believe in.

Is He here, or is there another like Him? My doubting thoughts began to turn my clothes grey.

I got the answer straight away. She said:

—Your Christ is also our Son, but he doesn't speak your language. Here He is called the Blossom Son. Here He doesn't need to suffer as on the earth. He has released us from the bonds of our planet.

He is the Son of all the worlds, all the kingdoms, over seas, forests, valleys and lakes. For him the wind subsides, the depths open, the mountains move, the flowers sing.

No one doubts who He is. Everyone knows. In your churches you have the Son hanging on a cross. The earth inhabitants were so terrible that they nailed Christ to a cross. When He lived on the earth He felt the same as other earth men. When He came to us His appearance was like ours. He felt like us here and He lived like us.

I see that you wonder why He came here, as we seem to live without sin.

No populated planet lives without sin; there's only more or less of it. Every planet needs its own Son. Our Blossom Son and your Christ is the same. He comes from eternity, He is eternity. He didn't tell you about all the worlds He visited. He hasn't told us either. Some things have to remain secret; otherwise there would not be life. Life is secret.

I wonder about the picture hanging in the far corner of the temple, a picture in a dim light.

—Yes, it is the Blossom Son, who cries over all the dark thought-garments created by the blossom beings. Every tear that drips down his cheek feels like a bullet. It is a picture to remind everyone about who gave them their beautiful garments, who gave them freedom.

One day he will return and give completeness.

—At every festival for Blossom Father the Blossom Son is there, so everyone can see the light of His soul. No one can touch Him, that is the only thing that is different from the time he was born here, or, rather, when he came here.

We don't die here or get born like you do on Earth. We are far, far closer to what you call 'the other side'. What you call 'to die', is here a mere change of dwelling. There is an even greater peace than here. More beautiful music. There is even more beautiful art work amidst the flowers and trees and even more faith in each being's littleness.

And this you should know, you little one from the human realm. The Blossom Son did not suffer when He was with us in the way He did with you. I do not blame you. You did not know any better.

Don't think now that all planets have inhabitants like us. Some planets are bare and empty. It looks as though nothing can grow. But it isn't always what it looks like. There is life but you and I can't see it. Life is everywhere.

It's called natural life, neither high nor low, all decided on by Blossom Father when he decided Everything.

Haven't you noticed how, on the earth where you dwell, much appears lifeless but nevertheless is full of life?

Haven't you seen how the fire in its mighty living power throws life over its dark surroundings? How many ponder over what fire is? Is it something an earth person invented a long time ago? Is that right? No! Fire was not invented. It was. It can be called forth in many ways.

It is fire itself that is life. Life that is never extinguished. The flames dwindle, but the life within the fire is always hidden in nature. What you call 'nature' we call 'blossomadamha'. It means 'from the first day of life'.

You wonder where we get our money from.

What should we do with money? Here everything is free, nobody owns anything. Everything is loaned. But we have to pay a price, not with money, but with our soul. We pay for our freedom with our own soul and we do that with our most beautiful soul colours. Sometimes it's hard to create only pure light colours. You have to be them, not just wish for them.

You wonder if we ever have disagreements?

Listen, we who live here have overcome our differences. We long to live in harmony. We see who wants to do the right thing. There are other places for those who don't want to live here. Free will is owned by everyone.

Do you wonder what we eat? We are nourished by everything; from the sea, the air, the music, the scents.

How do we live? In blossom houses with our friends.

And our work? To do the good, to think thoughts that give our neighbours beautiful pictures to look at. Sometimes we bring little childish earth people to show them our dream reality. The little earth people may see their own grey world full of strife, unwillingness and the mundane. The earth person can bring back some of the real light—the light that is lit by the living Lord of Light.

How do we die?
We don't die. We merely move to another dwelling outside this one. We can still be together as we are not separated. There is no sorrow, only joy.
Here exists joy and faith. That's why things happen the way they do.
We believe everything. Our Blossom Father, who is your God, performs miracles. We see them and that's why we believe in them.

You wonder if any dark powers come here? They are everywhere. But they have one great weakness, they can't stand the light. It makes them blind, and that's why we must keep the light of this kingdom so clear that no evil powers will want to live here. There is no illness, as the Blossom Son released us from it.

Use your free will in a right way.

Don't think, little earthling, that we are proud about our elevated position.

We would be nothing without Blossom Father and no light would exist without the Blossom Son.

We would be smaller than the earth's smallest grain of sand.

We are almost nothing in Blossom Father's great eternity, but we know it.

Blossom Father hears prayers from everyone and everything we ask for we get. Therefore it is difficult not to ask for too much.

I shall tell you, little earthling, how it can be if you ask for too much.

The Blossom Kingdom Legend

A poor woman was sent by a good fairy to the Blossom Kingdom. The good fairy took the woman there, but she didn't explain the Blossom Kingdom law to her.

The woman thought she had reached Paradise and for the first time she lived as if in complete bliss.

How easy it was to get everything. She only had to wish and everything came immediately. She asked for everything and everything came, like a miracle. In the end she was a prisoner of all the things she'd wished for. Everything was around her, under her, surrounding her and she never had time to use what she was given. It was only a bother.

She longed to return to the poor world where she often had to wait many many years before she got what she wished for, and sometimes she didn't get it at all.

She had been much happier than now, with all this splendour which was drowning her. But nothing stands still.

Finally, the poor woman was freed from her

possessions. She had, of course, wished for them herself, but she hadn't understood that the Blossom Kingdom had its own natural laws.

In memory of the poor woman there is a whole town which remains full of all her wished-for treasures. That is the museum of the Blossom Kingdom and everyone can go there along a narrow path to see it for themselves. Every room is full of expensive and beautiful things and it's very interesting to see.

There are things that a little earthling could never even dream about. Everything is made from the most beautiful diamonds, from shining gold and gleaming crystals.

Surprised, I asked about where she kept her bed.

—There, by the wall, I was told, but the bed was full of treasures and there was no place for the woman to live.

She wasn't a nasty being. Where is the woman, I wondered?

—She has gone to another place in another world where she can carry on living.

—She had turned up too early in the Blossom Kingdom, and next time when she comes she will not ask for more than she needs.

Everyone should be allowed to make mistakes—even the beings of the Blossom Kingdom.

On the earth people become enemies. They can't stand each other's faults. The Blossom Son, who is also your Christ, said, 'Love your enemies.'

He loved everyone. He was the light. Here in the Blossom Kingdom we have gone in that direction. But you, little earthlings, you have been given a mind in order to find the light.

You are surprised that we don't have books to read from.

Our own thought ego is our book. No one here needs to believe in anything somebody else has thought, said or written. We are so highly developed that we can perceive what the earth beings are only guessing or wondering about.

We perceive the laws of eternity in all our senses.

We want to be united with Blossom Father and with the Blossom Son.

We have transcended what you call 'the cold hand of death' and we only want to see 'the warm hand of life'.

Our greatest light is our love towards our known and unknown friends, who are everywhere.

On the earth you think God wants revenge! And that when He is angry He will punish you.

Do you know why you think that, little earth pebble?

Only because you yourself want revenge, are evil and spoiling for a fight. You demand that those who have treated you badly shall shout: 'Sorry, sorry!' How limited you are in your perceptions!

You give your God the same abilities as you yourself have acquired through your own sin.

Power rules amongst you. Evil power.

The one who dominates wins.

But your earthly power is worthless.

You think God likes what you yourself like. Poor little earth creatures!

You think that if they sin God throws his children into something you call the eternal fire.

It is right that there is an eternal fire but that fire isn't evil. Everything that our Blossom Father has created is good. Everything has been given to be used.

How do the people of the earth use fire?

Part of the fire they call eternal Hell. Part of it the eternal Paradise. In this way they hold two earth Bibles in their hands, the Bible of Life and the Bible of Death.

There should only be one kind of Bible, the Bible of Truth. That is written by the Highest himself.

We also have a Bible. Everything is written down in the Bible of the Blossom Kingdom. In it we read the will of the Blossom Father.

You earth dwellers also have that Bible.

It was meant from the beginning that only a single

Bible would exist. Everyone could read it. Everyone could understand it, but that is not how it turned out.

Do you know what your word 'religion' means? It means nature. Nature means religion.

Here in the Blossom Kingdom we know ourselves.

But no one with you knows themselves. You always think something different. Some of you think you're better than you are. Some think they're worse.

Nobody thinks the right thing.

Nature is purely spirit life, wholly spirit life.

But what is spirit life? It is that life which made the beings of the Blossom Kingdom into what they are. What is life? With us it is Blossom Father, your God.

Not all earth humans are blind to the miracles of nature. There have been many great seeing earth dwellers.

Do you remember Topelius? He has visited us here in the Blossom Kingdom. He was told the story about Sálami and Zúlamit.

I still remember it. Would you like to hear it, little earth child?

> Far away on a star he lived
> in the beauty of the sky.
> She lived on another sun

and in a different region
her name was Sálami and his was Zúlamit.

Both had noble love
and loved each other already on the earth.
But parted by the night
and death and sorrow and sin,
quickly they grew white wings
there in the realm of death
they were judged to live on separate stars
far from each other
in their blue vaulted homes
they thought about each other.

An infinite space of lustre
and suns lay between them.
Speechless worlds, miracles
of the creator's hand,
lay between the lives
of Sálami and Zúlamit.

One night Zúlamit's power of longing
became unbearable
So he began to build
a bridge of light from world to world;
and Sálami, began like him

to build from the edge of her sun
a bridge from world to world.

For a thousand years
with inestimable faith they built,
and so the Milky Way appeared,
a shimmering star-bridge,
encompassing the highest heavenly vault
and the zodiac's path
Binding together
the shores of oceans' spaces.

The bridge was finished
and Sálami and Zúlamit
ran into each other's arms—
and straight away a clear star,
clearest in the vault of heaven,
rose up before their way.
After a thousand years of sorrow
the heart bursts into bloom.

And all who on the dim earth
have loved tenderly and gladly
who have been parted
by sin and sorrow, by doubt
and death and night,

will win the power
to build a bridge from world to world.
Love will be reached
and longing find peace.

Yes, this was a beautiful tale
of infinite great love
Even on the earth
there are little children
who believe in fairy tales
So Zúlamit and Sálami got help
from the fairy of the tale
so they could build
a star-bridge in fairyland.

There we will find Zúlamit
and Sálami his friend
living in a beautiful dwelling
in star heaven
Never to be parted again
little children from the cold earth
their Bible always was
the Highest words of promise.

So, dear little earth children
have faith like Zúlamit
then your thoughts will turn
light angel-white
and Sálami will surely
reach out her hand
so even you one day
will find the land of stars.

—Yes, these were fine verses you read, Blossom Fairy; some I recognized, but not all.

—It may have something to do with the author composing the last three verses only when he came to the Blossom Kingdom, so you are the first earth being who hears them.

Maybe you want to hear a song that no one outside the Blossom Kingdom has heard.

—Yes, I would like that.

The Blossom Goddess sang for me, but I can only write down the words.

The Blossom Kingdom Song

In the Blossom Kingdom there is peace
given by Blossom Kingdom time
the peace which Light has given us is colours
Blossom Kingdom's children,
the children that Blossom Father had chose.

And Blossom Son came to us
to our kingdom
where there is no one like him
his whole body was a soul
he came and suffered for everyone,
so Blossom children should not
fall back into sinful ways.

That's why we sing our praise
with thoughts, and not with tongues
to celebrate the Highest Father.
Little earthling
listen to the Blossom Kingdom words
about how it is in Blossom Kingdom.

Here you find no illness and no pain
no low thoughts as you have on earth,
there where are also war and terror

and many are dressed in tatters.
Tell me what earth life teaches you?

I listened with stillness to the song and music which reached me like colour cascades. I have no earthly words to describe how I heard it, I am only a mere earth creature who can't think pure or even less speak and write pure.

But I will still try to write down the Blossom Kingdom's story as I heard it.

The Blossom Goddess continues:
—You little earth dwellers, you are so frightened of everything. Why is that?

You are afraid of different kinds of weathers. Afraid of animals, of illness, of slander. Yes, you are afraid of each other.

Fear ties you up with its own bands, round your whole body. You can't see them yourself, but I am telling you so that you will see them.

I looked at myself. I didn't feel tied up and I told her so.

—Not now, not here. You can't be tied up here by your earthly fear, for you are in the Blossom Kingdom, but when you return to the earth this fear will come back.

—But I am not afraid of everything!

The Blossom Goddess looked at me and smiled.

–Is it so difficult to be an earth dweller?

I thought we were doing pretty well on Earth.

But I must confess that everything felt easier now. Nothing resisted, everything was free.

But how shall we have to be on the earth, to have it like this?

Immediately the Blossom Being perceived my thought, because the answer came straight away.

–Stop playing up. It is the way that you are playing up that holds you imprisoned.

–Please, Blossom Kingdom Being, teach me how we shall live on the earth so we can become like Blossom Kingdom Beings. Help me so I can help the earth dwellers when I go back.

–I will not write any laws for you, little one, only tell you the eternal Blossom Kingdom tradition.

It starts with love. Have love towards everything. People, animals, flowers, the Sun, the Moon, Stars, rain, storm, everything, everything!

Love is the greatest thing Blossom Father has created. It has the biggest part in everything. Use freedom correctly.

What does that mean, you wonder. Through love you will know how to use freedom correctly.

Stop worrying. How, you're asking.

Now you have learned to use freedom through the tradition of love, how can you then worry when you feel freedom?

If you are in a place which makes you worry, go away. Freedom will help you.

Believe in everything that is beautiful and true.

How, you wonder—I cannot believe in most of the things that are beautiful and true, when so many things are ugly lies.

—Earth child, we had come so far that you had thought away fear and worry.

So why are you still worried about ugliness and the lies of the earth?

See friends in everyone you meet.

—But maybe those I meet want to harm me. They may look nice and kind, but really they are nasty and evil.

—Have you already forgotten that you thought away ugliness and lies?

Little earth child, in this way we can continue to think away everything that is unpleasant and ugly.

But your head can't take any more. If you teach your earth friends all I've told you your earth will be much happier. Maybe it won't happen at once but bit by bit it will get better. Don't forget that you must remain child-like. You must believe in fairy tales, in miracles, in love. In the beautiful. In the pure.

Don't read anything soiled! Your thoughts will be soiled.
Don't see anything soiled! Your eyes will be soiled.
Don't hear anything soiled! Your ears will be soiled.
Don't eat anything soiled! Your stomach will be soiled.
Don't speak anything soiled! Your mouth will be soiled.
Don't think anything soiled! Your soul will be soiled.

Little earth dwellers, you have a long way to go before you reach the light, but live according to the tradition of the Blossom Kingdom and then the light will come sooner.

It is not as difficult as you think.

–Perhaps not difficult here, Blossom Kingdom Goddess, but it's almost impossible on the earth.

–Why is it impossible on the earth, little earth child? You are industrious! Begin with only thinking kind thoughts. It won't take long until you start to speak kind words. When you speak kind words to humans, they will begin to think kind thoughts and when they speak kind words it will be followed by kind deeds. So slowly it will go, bit by bit. Everything must first come into the human soul through the head, which has first to think the good.

Then it will not be so difficult for the body to do what the soul has thought out in the head. But if the soul has thought evil thoughts, then the human body will do evil. It's easy to grasp that, isn't it?

Little earth child, when you return to the human earth, don't forget the Blossom Kingdom story, take it with you, teach it to the sad little earth children. Not everyone will listen, as they must have a wise childlike brain in order to understand. If they only have an intellectual adult mind they won't have time to listen.

But earth child, don't lose your patience. Think about the light which is there beyond the grey clouds. That light will help you to throw glimmers of light over the darkness. It will help you see the starry world, so large, so enormous, so wonderful, which only 'awake' beings can see.

In time the earth inhabitants will see each other as they really are.

They will see each other's soul colours. Colours which immediately reveal lies.

It will take a long time but it will happen.

Don't forget what you've learnt.

I will give you a verse to give to the earth beings. Read it to them!

The Blossom Kingdom sends greetings to the earth
a greeting, with an abundance of light,
which rays past endless starry worlds
it will reach to every earth dweller
throw away nasty anger

throw away thoughts of murder,
throw away all jealousy and meanness,
listen to the words of the Blossom Kingdom.

Think goodness of everyone and everything
think how you yourself want to be met
think health towards all who are ill
think life in everything that has died
only think good thoughts
think everything in utmost humility
think that you yourself are little
think light forever.

—I will try to remember the poem, Blossom Goddess, and try to write it so that little earth children can read it.

—Now little earth child, you can not stay here in the Blossom Kingdom any longer. You must go back to your planet.

I will accompany you on your journey. Get ready so we can travel.

The moment had arrived to leave. It felt difficult to leave all the beauty.

But I had only been promised a moment in the Blossom Kingdom.

I thanked the Blossom Goddess for everything I had experienced.

We started the return journey. It went with the same breath-taking speed. Past the star worlds, some bare, some green with blue oceans and large, large forests with trees which looked like giant palms, some stars, flowering just like in the Blossom Kingdom, some with high mountains or large desolate lands with strange inhabitants looking like our apes, but larger, clumsier. Some worlds where war was raging, with death and misery, terrible, terrible!

I was glad that journey went so fast. I could neither see the beauty in the beautiful nor the terrible in the ugly.

So I had returned to the earth and the Blossom Goddess went back to her Kingdom.

It took a while until my thoughts got used to the earth.

I thought through everything I had encountered, everything beautiful I'd seen, everything beautiful I had experienced.

Could the earth really be like that if we wanted it?

But what about all the planets we went past that had it much worse than us? Why was it so different in the different worlds?

God surely wished well for his children, wherever he sent them.

Should I dare to tell the Blossom Kingdom tale to the earth humans?

I thought it would be a good idea to tell a little bit to my best friend. She listened for a while but it didn't take long until she said:

–You are out of your mind! You cannot expect me to believe that.

What did I mean? I don't know. I only wanted to tell her what I had experienced.

My friend went off, looking at me with eyes of pity.

–'Poor you,' she said before the door slammed shut behind her.

Perhaps I could dare to tell my parents.

They listened, and when I had finished they said:

–Your imagination certainly sets the mind in motion! It's a good fairy tale.

I was glad. No one needs to see it as anything other than a fairy tale. A fine fairy tale, which will perhaps help people towards a kinder reality. A fairy tale-reality.

Should I dare to write a book about the fairy tale?

Would people think that I was strange?–But would it matter what they thought? Not at all!

I think the earth can also become a Blossom Kingdom.

I believe that people can learn to be kinder.

So kind that it wouldn't matter if you could see their thoughts.

I want to tell the whole world that I believe in a Blossom Kingdom, also for us.

I want to go round to people and tell the Blossom Kingdom story. Not everyone will laugh at me. Maybe there are many childlike people? Maybe I would succeed?

First, I told it in my own land. Some listened, some didn't. Some laughed, some smiled, thinking, 'She's out of her mind.'

I came to our neighbouring country. They listened and no one laughed. They wanted the book of the Blossom Kingdom. They longed to have their own Blossom Kingdom. I promised to write the story of the Blossom Kingdom and send it to them.

There were many childlike, wise people. Maybe they had met cruelty more closely and therefore they longed more.

I travelled further and came to a great country and there I told them my story.

But everyone was in a hurry. Everyone was afraid of a new world war. No one had time for stories.

They needed to make weapons. They were only clever. There was no human childishness. Only cold grown-up thoughts of war, death, money and power. There was no place for even a small flower, and even less for a whole Blossom Kingdom story.

I travelled on to the land of the black people. I wanted to call it the thought-land of light. Many there already knew the tale of the Blossom Kingdom. They listened and smiled, though not at me but with me. They longed for the tale to become reality. Their black faces were shimmering with light. I guessed that it was their beautiful thoughts which coloured their faces with light. These black people were happy in themselves. They liked to sing.

They had their own faith which helped them to see life in light colours.

> *My black skin who created it?*
> *It was the God of Heaven,*
> *still we are laughed at*
> *but the colour is God's making.*
> *Myself I am not sad*
> *I have light in my soul*
> *and song comes out of my throat*
> *despite being a slave to toil.*

The black people, they sang a lot. The black skin gleamed, the teeth gleamed, the eyes sparkled. How could they be so happy?

Could they perhaps see past the earth's dreariness? Did they not need as much food and clothing as us to feel happy?

I thought of the music and song of the Blossom Kingdom. Wasn't the blacks' song related to that?

The music in the Blossom Kingdom formed a beautiful coloured cloud which left behind wonderful melodies as long as a little cloud of music remained in the sky.

It was the same with the song. It left fine coloured cloud banks that slowly sailed across and gradually disappeared into lighter and lighter colours.

Maybe it was because of this that these people understood the Blossom Kingdom tale.

Think how eagerly they decorated themselves with flowers.

More and more I began to grasp the life of the black ones.

They were also not as scared of death as their white relatives.

Inwardly, they knew they didn't stop living just because they came to another world.

Maybe they had lifted a bit of the veil which hangs between our world and the other one.

Maybe they had come a bit of the way towards the Blossom Kingdom?

I became more and more interested in the black people with the light souls.

'*What does it matter if a hand is black when it is honestly stretched out!*'

Think how much is said in a few words. How many can stretch their hands out honestly?

Many stretch out their arms to receive gifts, and many pretend a friendly greeting, many speak so much with their hands that they can't speak with their mouths; that is pretence. There are many ways to stretch out your hands.

I suddenly thought of the pictures I'd seen of Jesus. He is often pictured with His arms out as if He wants to embrace everyone.

Jesus never raised His hand or arm as a threat against anyone or anything. He who created arms, hands and everything, surely He did not want them to be used as a threat against anyone. No, for certain He meant that they should be used as a help for everything.

I wonder if people really think how grateful they should be that we have arms and hands.

Think if we were suddenly without arms? It is ghastly and frightening to think about that.

You say, why should we think about that?

Well, there is so much we can do with our arms.

Here on the earth it is not yet a Blossom Kingdom, so we can think about everything we want with our thoughts. We must also use our arms as well as our thoughts.

Say why you think that you are graced
to have two hands so beautiful
You can write a letter
You can fold them in prayer.

You can give a little caress
You can carry burdens
and be happy even when you are in trouble
if a friend's hand comforts you.

With hands you can build again
what was laid to waste
Give your hand to the one who suffers
this is what the Lord Himself has said.

I now look on the earth and on its people in a different way than I did before I experienced the tale of the Blossom Kingdom.

Think how beautifully human beings have been created. No machine in the whole world can be compared to them.

If only the people could stop, look around, listen to the music of nature, see how everything is alive. See how trees and flowers are alive. If you really look you can see how the petals branch out in small fine nerve threads throughout the whole flower. You can feel precisely how the plant also has senses.

Maybe my soul eyes had awakened after my journey to the Blossom Kingdom.

I could sit for long periods of time with my eyes shut. In my inner vision I could see large expansive fields, green, verdant grass, golden skies, translucent water. Colours that gently float, not fast but unnoticeably with colours changing into one another.

Surely, everyone could slow down a little, and look inside into their own fairy tale world.

I dare to write this, as you who have read this far must like fairy tales, otherwise you would have given up long ago.

Wouldn't you sometimes like to sit down alone, alone with your thoughts, and ponder on the meaning of our life on the earth?

Surely, it can't be the intention that a load of wise, less wise, healthy, sick, beautiful, ugly, kind or nasty beings shall rush around as if they were half-blind and half-deaf.

God has given us so much beauty, but how can we use it when so many people can't even see it?

Human beings' empty emptiness
is not the emptiness of life

no, it is the emptiness of human beings
who do not learn from life
they go along so dull and lonely
with lowered eyelids
like the animals in a large herd
that is chewing the grass.

They move along
and are virtually asleep
everything is the same to me
they think as they walk
along their earthly path
they don't want to be awake
they don't want to be glad
they don't hear the song of the birds
they don't see the leaves on the tree.

But some are awake
and see God's beautiful world
they see the miracles on the earth
they are taught by nature
they listen to the birdsong
in the raindrops they see an earth
an earth full of beauty
given by the Lord Himself.

> *These human beings are rich*
> *from the wealth of their souls*
> *they see life in everything*
> *they do not speak of death*
> *they are so wise in a childish way*
> *believing in tales*
> *this is just a greeting*
> *as a gift from nature.*

Sometimes I wonder why everyone is in such a hurry. There is plenty of time, an eternity in fact.

I suddenly think of wise sayings I read somewhere. They fit so well that I'll write them here.

> *Most people can't feel. They only think they feel. They don't believe. They only think they believe.*
> *If you want others to believe in you, then believe in yourself. Believe in the goodness that is in you. There are others who will believe that evil is in you.*
> *Don't rush after what you see as beautiful, it will always be there in front of you.*
> *Don't shout for God. He can read your innermost thoughts.*

Maybe you ask, 'But where is God? Surely, you must shout aloud, to the one you can't see'.

You cannot see the whole of God at one time.

—Do you know why? We're only human beings and we can't understand everything. Much of what we can understand we don't want to.

It's like the little mouse who sees bits of food around the rubbish bin. She looks this way and that, all around the bin. She thinks she and the leftovers are the only things in life, in her mouse life. She's a lonely little mouse, without friends, without family. If she had understood that there are loads of other rubbish bins and other food she wouldn't have risked her life just to reach that bin and those leftovers.

But the little mouse couldn't understand anything more than this. If she were curious and wanted to know more, one day she would find a better rubbish bin with better leftovers.

I often think of the Blossom Kingdom and the Blossom Kingdom Goddess.

I asked her, in the same way as you who are maybe reading what I write, 'But where is God?'

She answered, 'Shall I tell you, little earth child?'

I wanted this very much. I asked again and Blossom Goddess answered.

Where Is God?

What are the oceans and all the rivers?
Yes, they are the blood of Father God!
What is the sun that always shines?
Yes, it is the warmth of the Lord's Being!
But what is the moon and all the stars?
Yes, they are the cells of the Lord's Body!

But what is fruit, with all the seeds?
That is nature with eternal hope!
But what is time that never stands still?
That is an infinite eternity!
What is sorrow that hurts us?
Yes, that is the evil of vanity!

If people knew what is good for them
and simply saw a friend in everything,
if they did not look jealously at their neighbour
if they simply did what God commanded.
But God is the ocean and all the winds
As well as stars and mother sun!

But how can I constantly obey
if I cannot find my God in His chair?
So little you are, human being,

you want to find God, but you don't know how.
Silence I will whisper, open your window
there is God, in His nature.

If only you would look you would see His hand
at each one's side.
See great forests, and wide meadows
See mountains so big, see flowering land!
Everything is the Lord, large and beautiful!
Here the birds sing and the brook rushes!
Fold your hands in a wordless prayer
you are walking around in your Father's house!
Don't ever again say, you cannot find the Lord.
All we human beings have to do is remember
God our Father is in everything we see!

I was silent for a long time after the Blossom Goddess had spoken. *Everything* was God!

My poor, poor head was aching. Maybe it was because the thoughts in there had something to do, even the laziest thoughts. I imagined that even the smallest and silliest thoughts could begin to work. Grand thoughts which rarely or never wanted to move were suddenly raring to go. Hadn't they missed out on an awful lot? Surely it isn't a good life for clever fine thoughts, just to lie down and be lazy.

Suddenly, I felt so happy. Grateful—towards God,

towards the Blossom Goddess. She has reached my innermost thoughts—the grand kingdom in me, which is also the lofty kingdom. The thought kingdom which was entirely satisfied with its own lofty empire. Out of myself I would never have reached to this.

Many will say, how silly you are, because that kingdom is part of yourself!

I know that, but all beings consist of different kingdoms. Kingdoms which you don't know about. You can also say, many 'I's. How many of your own 'I's does a human being know? You have 'I's that you never even knew existed. Think how many times you say and do something and later on you think about what you did. Then you say, 'How could I have said or done that?'

That's when one of the 'I's or the kingdoms inside had come forward and made a decision. An 'I' that you didn't know about. Isn't it awful. Terribly awful. Think, if you had already known all your 'I's, then you wouldn't have let that 'I' hurt both yourself and others.

War and terror will continue in the world as long as the human beings don't know all their 'I's.

Those who govern the land also have many unknown 'I's inside them. If they are peaceful and good unknown 'I's, then nothing dangerous will happen. In fact it will be the opposite. But if they have warmongery and nasty 'I's, then it is very dangerous. That's why it's important, very important, that human beings try to discover their own kingdom, the human kingdom. Those who do not know their own kingdom have nothing to teach others.

In the Blossom Kingdom everybody knows completely their own 'I'. They have reached much further than we earth human beings. They dared to show their 'I's. Just like when an earth person blows out the smoke, when she breathes out cigarette smoke, so do the Blossom People breathe out their 'I' clouds. They come in different colours according to what they think.

Nobody wants to think bad thoughts when everybody can see them. Everyone wants to send out as many beautiful 'I' clouds as possible. The more beautiful the 'I', the more beautiful the cloud. The 'I' cloud forms their clothes as I've told you before.

It would be quite awful if all the people here on earth were to exhale their human 'I's as a cloud of smoke. You would only see a foggy, dark grey cloud. Here and there it would be almost black. In one or the other place it would shine in fine colours, as the earth also has many fine citizens. There are those who know about some of their own kingdoms but are scared of their unknown ones. Still they try to become friends with their unknown selves.

Just now, at this moment, I hear beautiful music, Handel's concerto for organ, opus 4 in F Major. It seems as if the notes come to me in large light streams, every note having a different colour. Now comes more music–Swan Lake. I wish my words could describe what I feel.

What does my innermost music-'I' look like? How was music born; did it appear like a newborn baby or was it already in space before the world began?

I think everything has music inside it. When you walk in the forest you can hear a thousand different voices. Voices which float into each other. There is no disharmony between the notes, they simply float in and out, unnoticed and still. Only when you are alone with nature can you listen to the world's deep music, which leads your thoughts to Paradise or to the Blossom Kingdom. Surely, we can have something of the life in the Blossom Kingdom here on earth.

We can actually see coloured light around everything which is alive. Have you ever thought about how different it feels, being together with different people? Surely you can feel the colours round those you are together with. Perhaps not clearly, but you can sense it if you think enough about it. Maybe I experience life and the world in my very own way. This I have understood since I was little. I remember the first time I really thought. It was just before I started school. Some friends and I were by the seashore. The big enormous ocean lay before us. Large rocks, sandy beach, stones, driftwood, seagulls circling over the water, a little swallow or sparrow drifted past—a part of the universe.

I shall tell you why I suddenly understood maybe why I was different. I experienced that I was one with nature, one with the universe, one with the large wonderful existence of worlds.

Suddenly such a feeling of happiness existed within me. One of the girls said, 'Shall we go home, I'm not enjoying this any more.'

After a while I left them. I just felt I couldn't go on with them.

'Not enjoying this any more', she had said. How could she say that? I started to wonder why she said that. Didn't she see the mighty ocean, the blue sky and the feathery clouds? Or the seagulls' proud flight? Or the little mussel which had been thrown up on the shore? Or the damp sand formed like little waves?

Everything had its own tale to tell. I remember how I sat down alone on the beach; everyone had gone home. I experienced minutes of eternity. It felt as though the whole of nature gave me its innermost being. The lapping of the waves was just like my own heartbeat. The little mussel lay at my feet and I stood up, took the mussel and put it back in the water, back into its own world. I took a handful of wet sand, I talked to the sandgrains, I felt that they also were one with nature. I felt peace, love, communion with all.

The Sun started to go down, everything mixing its colours, the Sun, the heavens, the ocean. Everything became a oneness. I, a little human being, was allowed to take part in this incomprehensibly beautiful tale. I remember that I looked around me. I looked and felt and lived, I felt in communion with it all. I had bare feet, I felt the damp sand beneath them. Felt the earth's own warm life as I walked on the beach. I felt as if I was wandering over the whole earth, felt as if I was looking, but what was there to look for? I had just found everything in this large incomprehensible eternity that is—now! Could beauty become bigger and more beautiful? Could peace become more whole?

No, but I shall tell you what I was looking for. It was a longing that just came. It was just there inside me. It was in my head, in my heart. Yes, in me, in my hands and in my feet. I looked for someone whom I could share all these experiences with. Someone who could come to me just like the whole of nature had come to me.

I felt myself separated from the human world.

I remember how my thoughts shaped themselves within me, how I grasped that this was a large and un-understandable gift that I had been given as a birthday present, to open my senses to everything that is unearthly and beautiful. I felt that I became conscious of higher worlds where everyone could live in peace and beauty, where everyone could see the real life.

From the universe I perceived a voice which came to me in the form of music. It was as if the voice said: You little earth child, our Father has many dwellings. In those dwellings beauty never disappears. Some humans will see glimpses of beauty already on the earth, just like the beauty you have seen and experienced. The music voice from the cosmos told me of the Blossom Kingdom, of uncountable beautiful worlds. As I was strolling on this fine beach I promised the voice I would one day write the Blossom Kingdom story. I would write about all the beauty of all life, of all the experiences that had come to me. But always, always I looked for someone to share my thoughts with. I felt as if I was on a constant search, always expecting to find another searcher who could speak the same language as me. I knew that I would. I felt this certainty within me. I searched in the skies of heaven, in the stars, the ocean, everywhere I searched. I listened to the sound of the wind.

Shall I tell you where I found what I was looking for? I found it on the ground. I found footprints, footprints of bare feet, footprints which had walked on the naked beach. Someone else was also out walking. Someone who was also searching. The footprints became clearer and clearer. They were almost new. It couldn't have been long since the wanderer had made them.

Then I caught up with the wanderer. He who had walked before me. All of a sudden I could see him on the horizon. He heard the sounds of my steps. He stood still. He waited for me.

For a long time we just looked at each other, quiet, still, full of reverence. It was as if the whole of nature held its breath. The one who stood before me was Everything I hoped for. The one I had searched and waited for. He could tell me what was behind the Milky Way, behind the sea's unfathomable songs, behind the constant longing in the tiny human heart. He could tell me stories of the beauty of worlds. He gave comfort and peace to a little earth dweller. He told me He had always existed and that He always left footprints behind. He promised that I would feel His presence whenever I needed to. 'Perhaps I am not always visible to human eyes, but I exist in everything, both outside you and within you.'

Time was returning to my consciousness. I felt how the

world, the human world awoke in me anew. I looked around in bewilderment. He who had come from nowhere was not to be seen, but this was only for my outer eyes, as He was now within me.

I looked up and saw the last golden red sun-shimmer, which painted a beautiful picture for my outer and inner gazes.

There are moments in a human life that cannot be measured by earth inhabitants. There are no letters for forming some words, the words which shall be written only by the Almighty's own pen, the pen that doesn't know ordinary little words. It's a pen from the rainbow and the land of Heaven. The pen that is guided by the Highest hand. I am not sad that I don't own such a pen. No, only humbly grateful that I have been allowed to read what it has written. I can never have enough gratitude for that, though the owner of the pen doesn't ask for gratitude.

Now I think that everyone can learn to read what is written by this pen. You just have to adjust your eyes to a different writing than the letters of the alphabet. I don't know how to explain it. I was just given this gift freely, it just came to me.

The wandering man from the beach taught me about life's unfathomable beauty. He told me of the Eternal Life. Of truth, love and beauty. He promised to be there if

I was alone or sad. He promised to carry the world's beauty from eternity to eternity.

I wrote earlier that religion is nature. I also want to write that nature is music. I think that the greatest religion can reach people through music. There is music that corresponds to every little vein, every little nerve in the human body.

Haven't you heard countless times how after listening to music people can say, 'It shuddered through my whole body,' or 'That piece made me warm,' or 'It feels as though I'm in a different world.' Have you never wondered why music makes people want to dance? The greatest and finest music is only a reply from nature in space. There you find the raging of the autumn storm, the roaring of the waves, the spattering of rain and the songs of the birds.

There is an old legend which tells how Apollo made a lyre from seven holy stars.

Apollo, the Greek god, fetched the music from its own sphere. He had the ability to let the notes well forth out of the sphere of music. He just took the veil away. All real artists fetch their art from the treasure chest of the universe. There everything is genuine.

I want to reach into everyone. Maybe it will be easier to reach people with or through music. I think so. Yes, I think I know that. Sometimes little letters can be ruthless or merciless. They stand in a row on a sheet of paper, rigid and silent.

What can this say to people? Sometimes nothing. But I can listen to the notes of music from the high spheres, feel how everything has its own set melody, feel how everything gives an answer, a true answer. I wish I could give people something of what I have experienced. But the Blossom Goddess was right when she said that we small earth dwellers have tied ourselves up with our own bands, bands which neither let real life in or out. They just strangle the life spirit. They keep us here. In an earthly grip.

I often think of the Blossom Kingdom, the Wish Kingdom, the Fairy Kingdom. Unreal for many, but even more true for many.

Sometimes I don't know myself how to come to the innermost of life. The innermost meaning. Just when you think you have reached it or found it, it is suddenly miles away. Then everything is swept up by the grey reality, where strife, animosity, war and disaster plague the world.

But we must never forget that behind all this empty and sometimes terrible reality, there is a healthy, clean, immortal kernel which will never rot away.

It is that eternal kernel which will be there for eternity. To you who read this just now, maybe feeling sad, alone or sick, I want to whisper quietly and in stillness: don't be sad, don't forget the light which shines with strength in the eternal kernel! Everything is in a state of change. All shadows will be chased away by the light.

I wish that life's eternal light would enter every human soul. Everything good is light. Everything evil is dark. A human being has both light and darkness within.

We can call the light love and the darkness hate.

Nature is related to light, that's why nature is love. Religion and nature are also the same.

If you call on nature with love you will get a reply of love. If you call on nature with hatred you will get darkness and an answer of hate.

Remember the Blossom Goddess' words. Dark forces cannot stand the light. Couldn't we try to hold sway over the evil forces with the light of truth? Why can't we small earthlings help to make the earth a beautiful dwelling which is what its Owner intended from the beginning?

We can never demand that others should do things that we aren't willing to do ourselves. We always think: why should *I* do it? Somebody else can. When we think like that, nothing gets done.

Have you sometimes thought how large and fantastic it

is to have life? If you haven't thought that before, stop reading for a while and think. Do you know what you have in your possession? Yes, eternity! Eternity of good and evil. And you yourself decide what your eternity will look like.

Life is a walk over worlds in bare feet. You must go out in bare feet and get to know the earth thoroughly. The world's redeemer walked over the earth in bare feet, we are born with bare feet, we will leave the earth with bare feet:

Naked Feet

Feel earth, the naked feet
which searching go
feel earth, the bleeding feet
listen earth, to the feet
which wandered for days
which wandered through the night
two little naked feet
have written the song of life.

We have now entered
the kingdom of eternity
we wandered over kingdoms

to find life's answer
what did the little naked feet
find on the earth
did they find a world of joy?
did they find a world of murder?

Small little naked feet
tell in my book
tell of your wanderings
tell of the wise riddle of the world
write of the dangers of life
write what you know
small little naked feet
with little bleeding toes.

Why were human beings made with feet? Wasn't it so that they could wander through the kingdom of eternity, to return to God? Surely, it wasn't so that they would stand in the same place and look only at their immediate surroundings. No, they were created to wander, to discover God's wonderful world, to wander through deserts and luscious gardens, over war-torn countries and countries of peace, to see how people have changed God's beautiful creation. Everyone will learn something during their wandering. No wandering is the same. Some people will wander on the narrow path, even if there are cobble-stones or other obstructions, some try to take short-cuts to reach a beautiful goal, but most of all of those who wander will try and jump over all the bumps they meet.

Now I want to tell you what I know of the wandering. However we go or however we run, however we try to jump over all difficulties, everyone will at last find the only right way by not avoiding the obstacles or trying to take an easier route. No, everything is fair and just, and fair it will be when everyone has to do their bit.

You, who read this now, surely you think that God is fair? Of course, God is fair. He is fair. He judges fairly. Do you think that God punishes or rewards depending on the mood he's in? Do you think that God is some strict old uncle who sits somewhere up there and looks out at the world and counts faults and weaknesses according to how he feels? Surely you don't think that. Shall I tell you what I know? No, perhaps you say, how can she know more than I do? I'll change it and write the word 'believe', maybe it sounds better like that. Yes, that is better. 'This is what I believe in.'

Everything a human being says, thinks, does—yes, everything which flows out of the human being's body and soul, is reflected on the side where our Father lives.

There you find everything which ever happened on the earth. That is how God has shaped the natural law from the beginning. He gave human beings free will. What free will means can be understood by anyone who uses their brain properly. If you think that God is a large kind uncle, that's fine. But actually God is Everything, therefore He can also twinkle an eye secretly to you in your moments of loneliness, just like an old uncle.

He is the large murmering forest which sings its eternal song to all creatures. He is the stars which throw their twinkling light towards the earth. He is the snowflakes that slowly float to the earth and the little raindrops which hesitantly find their way down the windowpane. He is a piece of your mother and father, a piece of your grandma and grandpa, a piece of your sister and brother, a piece of your little child. He is also a piece of your friend and, don't forget, a piece of your enemy (if you have one).

Shall I tell you about one of the dreams I had one night?

Maybe you don't like dreams? Maybe you don't think they're real? But maybe dreams are real? And maybe reality is a dream?

Yes, I will tell you my dream.

I thought that everything suddenly stopped. Time stood still. Everything became so silent, so festive. I alone existed. Suddenly I saw a giant light. A light that became clearer and clearer. The light came closer and closer. So close that it completely enveloped me. Everything was still, everything at peace, complete. A voice reached my heart. A voice which was the light itself. The voice said: —My child, would you like to come on another journey? Now you have been in the Blossom Kingdom and seen how the small God-creatures live. Well, they were only the mirror reflection of good people's lives on the earth. Now you can follow the reflection of those people who have lived sinfully in the world, for there are uncountable dwellings of good and evil. I want to show you the evil counter-picture in the spiritual world. Come, give me your hand and I will show the way. One of my messengers will be your guide and explain everything.

Suddenly, the voice disappeared and an angel-like being held my hand. We went through the space. The light became less and less. We had arrived in a little kingdom, a little kingdom where everything was surrounded by a pale grey shimmer. There were some small grey houses here and there. The ground was meagre and full of stones. A few people went about with bent backs, working the soil. A few others were digging deep holes looking for water. I asked my companion:

—Which people are these? What are they doing? Why is everything so grey?

My companion answered:

—I will tell you about this. These are people who thought only about themselves during their wanderings. They were neither kind nor nasty but they only cared for themselves. They never gave anything away, not even anything of their abundance, but hung on greedily to what they owned. This is what their mirror image looks like, the life which they themselves built on the other side. They can find both water and food here, but it's hard work and very boring. They have themselves decided their future life.

Come, let us continue. And without being seen, we silently glided away.

With a sad feeling in my innermost being I left this grey kingdom, where not an ounce of sunshine lit up human existence.

Then we arrived at the next kingdom, it was even greyer, even duller. Here also were small houses but they were even more dilapidated. There were also people who had lived in the human world. Now they were alone, fettered to their chairs or beds. Full of longing, they looked through their small windows. But they had no possibility of reaching one another.

—What kind of people are these? I asked.

—These are the people who never bothered to visit, or even say a friendly word to the lonely and often sick people they met in their earthly wanderings. Now, they are having a taste of what it feels like to be treated as they treated their fellowmen. That is the way the holy law works.

We continued through endless kingdoms. The closer we got to the abyss, the worse it became. During our travels, we met worse and worse sinners. I cannot even write how robbers, murderers and people like that were living. I don't even think it could be printed.

Maybe someone, or many, wonder if my dream told about how it will be for these people? Or how long they have to stay in these dwellings?

In my next book I will tell about that.* The rest of my dream I will save, but already now I want to say that such an existence doesn't last forever. It will feel like an eternity for those who live there, but it isn't. God has not made laws which judge people and condemn them to eternal punishment.

God has not sentenced people to live in the dwellings I have written about. No, they themselves have built those dwellings through the way they lived on earth.

---

* This book was written but not published.

Maybe you wonder why I don't write the whole dream right now, but instead wait for the next book. But I have called this book 'A Moment in the Blossom Kingdom', so 'Dreams of the Abyss' would not be suitable here. Therefore, I will hide the rest till ᴍy next book. Maybe it will be called 'A Moment in the Abyss'.

Now, I think some people will say, 'What does she mean by the Blossom Kingdom, the Abyss and other similar words? Is she trying to invent her own new religion?'

'It can't be right what she writes.'

Some will say, 'Human beings are born and die, that's all there is to it.'

Some others will say, 'We are born but we never die, we just sleep a long sleep until we are woken on the last day.'

Anyone who can think can see that these thoughts are wrong.

The 'I' which is a human being, is not the visible physical body. The 'I' is the soul, and the soul is eternal. Then we know and understand that the soul can never die. In that case, the first thought I wrote above is wrong. Human beings can't be born and then just die for eternity.

Then comes the second thought, about being awakened on the day that people call the last day. What is it that shall be awoken? Is it the body, which is completely disintegrated? The body was only a momentary dwelling for the soul. So, it is impossible. Surely God doesn't need to use old disintegrated bodies and not bother to create new bodies.

So is it then the soul that should be awakened?

How can something be awoken that hasn't died? The soul *is* immortal!

I have heard it said at funerals, 'From ashes to ashes, dust to dust.'

It sounds ghastly. Awful. Undignified. I neither can nor am allowed to blame the priests who say this. They only say what they have been taught to say. I am sure there are many priests who would like to say something different. Many feel it is wrong to say this. I *know* it is wrong. Through my whole being it shouts: tell people what you know about life and death, give people comfort during their earthly wandering, spread some shimmering light over the endless desert of religion. Help people to understand how short one earthly life is.

God or Jesus never said the words: 'Ashes to ashes, dust to dust.' Never, I say.

I pray, or rather, I have a great humble prayer to the one who reads this and to those who have a lot to say within the church:

Take away those awful words. Change them and say instead: 'You go from life to life.'

I think I can promise you that everyone will feel more comforted by these words.

It was never the intention that science and knowledge of God should be a burden for human beings. That something that has to do with God should be boring. That people should stare blindly at everything that's been written about religion was never meant to be. All human beings have their own religion within them, even those who don't believe in God. They always believe in something, and the good they believe in is God or the good power. It does not matter which words I use. God is so easy to remember, because it's a word full of lightness.

Now, I want to say to you: don't be sad about what I write, as I only want to write down what I feel and think!

You can't believe or think with your body, it is through your soul that you have knowledge. My soul, as well as your soul, has come from God and that's why God's own thoughts are in my soul, and that is what I write.

God *is* sad about all the wrong doings that have come about on the earth. But, you say, why should we believe in what you write, maybe it doesn't come from God at all? Then I say to you: only believe in things you understand.

You have got heaven and hell within you, and you have got your own free will. God doesn't care about what you believe in. It is your actions and your way of living which is in His interest. One day everyone will realize how it really is.

It is much more fun to live if you are at least trying to comprehend God's great and wonderful goodness towards you.

I don't write to make people sad. Also not to earn money, or to be famous. It is of no interest if people know who I am. Surely, it's nice to be liked, you are then surrounded by many good thoughts and that helps to make life light.

If you are surrounded by bad thoughts, you get restless, nervous and listless.

You wonder, can thoughts have such an influence? Yes, and a thousand times yes! I want everyone to know that.

I know that many who read this understand the meaning of life. I know that there are many who have seen behind the veil of what is unknown.

I will write down part of the wise, fine words which great people have once written.

Maybe you've never read those pieces, therefore, I will write them here:

The human being is her own judge: if she is false, every-thing is false for her; if she is true, everything is true for her. It is a stupid thought to think: why isn't everyone as they should be? Those who grieve that they themselves are not what they ought to be, think wisely.

The present is a reflection of the past and the future is an echo of the present.

The one who doesn't know the truth is a child, the one who is searching for the truth has reached youth and the one who has found truth is an old soul.

> *Oh you who are Father*
> *over all that is created in heaven and earth*
> *open everyone's heart and let everyone hear your voice*
> *which always speaks within each human being*
> *reveal your Heavenly light*
> *which lies hidden in human souls*
> *send your godly Spirit's peace*
> *and unite all in love.*

I never meant to educate my fellow human beings, only to convey what I have seen and have knowledge of.

The moment I will leave the earth the numbers of you who have read my books will not make me proud. It is the thought that I have conveyed a message to so many searching souls that will comfort me, and the joy that I may have helped those in need will give me peace.

When it is difficult even for the worldly human being to live on the earth, how much more difficult must it be for the spiritual one?

The person who cannot keep a secret has no depth, he is like a bowl upside down.

The first truth one has to learn is to be true to oneself!

The one who makes room for others in his heart will find a dwelling everywhere.

Release me Lord from all the unfairness which comes from the bitterness of my enemies and from lack of knowledge from my beloved friends.

All these clever words were once said by a wise man.

I will finish this book now.
It has felt nice
and wonderful to write,
It was as though you had
been sitting here and listening
to the awkward letters
which are in my writing book.
I have not meant ill
to any human being

with what I've written,
I just wanted to write
and tell a little about the dream-world
which I sometimes experience,
I wanted to take you
with me for:

'a moment in the Blossom Kingdom'.

ALSO FROM CLAIRVIEW

AND THE WOLVES HOWLED
Fragments of Two Lifetimes
Barbro Karlén

'An extraordinary book ... deserves to be taken seriously.'
—*International Herald Tribune*

'A very thought provoking read! Whether or not she was really Anne Frank in another life, I do not doubt Karlén's sincerity.'
—Rabbi Yonassan Gershom, author of *Beyond the Ashes* and *From Ashes to Healing*.

For as long as she can remember, Barbro Karlén has harboured terrible memories of a previous existence on earth as the Jewish girl Anne Frank, author of the famous Diary. Until recently, she had kept this knowledge private. Now, prompted by a series of events which culminated in a struggle for her very survival, she is ready to tell her amazing story.

And the Wolves Howled is the autobiography of Barbro Karlén, from her early fame as a bestselling child literary sensation in her native Sweden, to her years as a policewoman and a successful dressage rider. But this is no ordinary life history. As the victim of discrimination, personal vendettas, media assassination, libel and attempted murder, Karlén is forced to fight for her very being. In the dramatic conclusion to her living nightmare, she is shown the karmic background to these events. She glimpses fragments of her former life, and begins to understand how forces of destiny reach over from the past into the present. With this knowledge she is finally free to be herself...

And the Wolves Howled is the story of one woman's superhuman struggle for truth in the face of discrimination and lies.

£10.95; 272pp (8pp b/w plates); ISBN 1 902636 18 X

A MESSAGE FOR HUMANITY
The Call of God's Angels at a Time of Global Crisis
K. Martin-Kuri

'Martin-Kuri acts as messenger for the angels and ultimately for their source, God... As angels transcend religious differences, so does this book. In it all people — religiously affiliated or not — may find heavenly inspiration and delight.'
— *Publishers Weekly*

Blessed with a special connection to the angelic hierarchies, K. Martin-Kuri relays this important 'message' for humanity at a critical time in our development. She reminds us of the many social crises which have brought us to the edge of the abyss. Now, at the dawn of the new millennium, we must either reach up to a better future, or stumble to the depths.

In *A Message for Humanity* Martin-Kuri translates into living practices the changes we can make to avoid disaster. She illumines the path of transformation that will allow our guardian angels to work more effectively in our lives and lead to change on a personal and cosmic level.

Every time we think a negative thought or commit an act of jealousy, greed or hatred, we are holding the angels at bay. The angels want to help us, but they are powerless, except in extreme cases, if we do not create an atmosphere of love and kindness in which they can intercede on our behalf. When God gave us free will, he gave us the opportunity to determine our fate. In hearing and acting upon the messages from the angels we can come closer to God.

Martin-Kuri shares with us special techniques for taming our inner dragons and defusing the powerful negative energies of society. She reveals how we can help ourselves and save our planet. Time is running out. The angels of God are calling. Will we hear their message? Will we make the right choice?

£9.95; 264pp; ISBN 1 902636 27 9

LIVING WITH INVISIBLE PEOPLE
A Karmic Autobiography
Jostein Saether

'The practical directness of Saether's descriptions is ingenious and stimulating, and they make reading the book exciting ... a contribution to research in the field of karma.'
— *Das Goetheanum*

After working methodically with meditative exercises for a number of years, Jostein Saether had a dramatic breakthrough. Sitting in his meditation chair, he experienced vivid inner pictures of an initiation ceremony in ancient Greece. He knew with absolute conviction that it related to one of his previous lives on earth. Continued meditative work led him to trace and research many of his past lives, which he relates in this extraordinary book. He also gives descriptions of many other spiritual experiences, and reflects on karmic investigation as an art and science.

Although nowadays many people are recalling memories of former lives on earth, few have followed the rigorous discipline of specific exercises in the way that Saether has. His work has enabled him to give vivid descriptions of past incarnations, and to show how they are present in metamorphosis in his current life.

Beginning with episodes from his present life leading up to his spiritual breakthrough, Saether takes us on a journey starting in the prehistoric ages of Lemuria and Atlantis, and on to the cultures of Egypt, Crete, India and Greece. He continues through early Christianity and the Middle Ages, up to the sixteenth and nineteenth centuries. A few well-known names appear along the way, as well as fascinating details that throw new light on known historical facts.

£14.95; 320pp; ISBN 1 902636 26 0

LIGHT BEYOND THE DARKNESS
How I Healed My Suicide Son After His Death
Doré Deverell
Foreword by George Ritchie

'An extraordinary book ... The best I have ever seen for people who have suffered through having a member of their family committing suicide.'
—George Ritchie, author of *Return from Tomorrow* and *Ordered to Return*.

Doré Deverell's son Richard had led a difficult life, plagued by physical and mental illness and depression. When he committed suicide at the age of 36, Doré was naturally devastated, suffering the intense anguish of a mother's loss. But she was determined to seek for healing and reconciliation.

This book is the first-hand account of how Doré Deverell made contact with Richard after his death. Encountering the work of the spiritual teacher Rudolf Steiner, she discovered methods by which she could communicate with her son's spirit. Suicides, she learnt, often experience great suffering and regret as a consequence of their premature death. But Doré was taught how to alleviate Richard's pain, and finally to metamorphose it. These practical steps are described here in an accessible way to aid anybody who finds themselves in a similar tragic situation.

In the unexpected conclusion to this extraordinary tale, Doré finds the person who, she believes, embodies Richard's reincarnated soul. Her work is rewarded with new hope, and Richard's soul is given a chance to learn and develop on earth once again.

Light Beyond the Darkness is a gripping account of love, despair, death and resurrection. Its central message—that, through the spirit, light overcomes dark—is a heartwarming confirmation of spiritual reality.

£8.95; 144pp; ISBN 1 902636 19 8

MY DESCENT INTO DEATH
And The Message Of Love Which Brought Me Back
Howard Storm
Afterword by George Ritchie

'For twenty years, I have been listening to and reading innumerable accounts of near-death experiences, but I have rarely
encountered one as powerful as Howard Storm's.
— Dr. Kenneth Ring, author of *Heading Toward Omega* and *Lessons
from the Light*.

For years Howard Storm lived the American dream. He had a fine
home, a family, and a successful career as an Art Professor and
painter. Then, without warning, he found himself in hospital in
excruciating pain, awaiting an emergency operation. He realised
with horror that his death was a real possibility, but as an atheist
he was convinced that his demise would mark the end of consciousness.

Storm was totally unprepared for what was to happen next. He
found himself out of his body, staring at his own physical form.
But this was no hallucination; he was fully aware and felt more
alive than ever before. In his spirit form, Storm was drawn into
fearsome realms of darkness and death, where he experienced the
terrible consequences of a life of selfishness and materialism.
However, his journey also took him into regions of light where he
conversed with angelic beings and the Lord of Light Himself,
who sent him back to live on earth with a message of love.

My Descent into Death is Howard Storm's full story: from his
near death experience in Paris to his full recovery back home in
the States, and the subsequent transformation of his life. Storm
also communicates what he learned in his conversations with
heavenly spiritual beings, revealing how the world will be in the
future, the real meaning of life, what happens when we die, the
role of angels, and much more. What he has to say will challenge
those who believe that human awareness ends with death.

£8.95; 184pp (8pp b/w plates); ISBN 1 902636 16 3

SEVEN STEPS TO ETERNITY
The True Story Of One Man's Journey Into The
Afterlife
as told to 'Psychic Surgeon' Stephen Turoff

'One of the best books of this genre to cross my desk in some time;
its easy style will be of equal appeal to experienced readers and
newcomers to spiritual matters alike.'
— *Psychic News*

'I died in the Battle of the Somme...' These were the astonishing
first words spoken to clairvoyant and healer Stephen Turoff by
the soul of James Legett, a young soldier who was killed in the
First World War. For two years, the world famous psychic surgeon communicated with the soldier's soul, and in the process
wrote down his remarkable story; not the tale of Legett's tragi-
cally short life on the physical plane, but of his death on a bat-
tlefield in France and his soul's subsequent journey into the
afterlife.

Although he works with many discarnate spirits in his clinic,
the dyslexic Turoff was initially reluctant to undertake the task of
writing a book. But he was persuaded by the boisterous and
genial soul of the dead man. Their literary collaboration involved
an unusual method: Legett presented spiritual pictures to Turoff,
who with clairvoyant perception interpreted them into words.
The result is this enlightening testimony of life beyond the illu-
sion of death, filled with insight, spiritual wisdom and delightful
humour. It is written to show that we are all eternal; there is no
death... only change.

£8.95; 192pp; ISBN 1 902636 17 1